THE GODSEND

THE GODSEND

BERNARD TAYLOR

St. Martin's Press New York

For Ricky and Bob

THE GODSEND

ONE

When it began there was no way of knowing that anything *had* begun. How could we know? Any of us? We had no sign. There was no drumroll, no great fanfare, no dramatic, soaring orchestra like you'd find in a Max Steiner film score. There was nothing; just a little silence. Her silence—surrounding her; a little look from us—and then Sam with his crumbs.

When enough time has passed perhaps I shall find it easier to look back, easier to speak of it all—and yet I wonder whether sufficient time could ever be. Right now there is no hour, no minute, when the thoughts and memories don't come pouring in. And they're too much to cope with. And when they do come they come unexpectedly, taking me off-guard, so that I'm left with no defence. So straight-away I start thinking of it all over and over again. Ceaselessly I find myself going through the chain of events—like tracing a circle—as if by doing so I could somehow rewrite the story. But it's always the same. There, before I know it, I'm where I am at the present—here, now. So I am led, link by link, to the start again, to begin over again, with the same beginning . . .

That summer.

I remember it as one of the warmest, brightest of summers; little rain; when Davie ran along the lane his feet kicked up tiny clouds of dust from the dry earth. But it was not parched, that season; the vivid green leaves and the soft grass were moist to my touch. It was a beautiful time. Perhaps later events have imbued it with a depth of charm and colour that was not there— but I don't believe so. It *was* beautiful.

I can see beauty, happiness and contentment manifested in myriad everyday sights and sounds: Kate, smiling as she sits feeding Matthew; the softness in her face; the gentle, but aggressive sounds from his tiny sucking mouth. The others running in and out of the house—Lucy, Davie and Sam. The shouts, the singing, the chasing, the laughter . . .

Now, glancing into the mirror I find it difficult to believe that so little time has gone by; my reflection tells a different story. But there, not time alone has taken its toll. Time is the minor exactor. And not only from me.

Here, where I sit, only silence comes from within the room, but outside the sound of the passing traffic drifts up to us. It's continuous, and there's no escape from it. I had thought I would get used to it in time. Now I realise I never shall. Before, the loudest sounds were birds' songs. You could stand by the plum-trees and hear the buzz of the wasps' wings as they settled on the over-ripe fruit. You could hear the rustling of the leaves. But that was *before*. That was *there*. That was *then*.

*　　*　　*

Having no boss to consult as to when I might take my summer holidays, Kate and I did the choosing, taking them when it suited us. And when July came up warm and sunny, this, we decided, was the time. And I relaxed. Two weeks away from the constant necessity to be creative. Two weeks away from pencils and paintbrushes. Two weeks away from deadlines. Nothing to think about but *us*—the family.

Because of the very tender age of Matthew, we didn't attempt any long visit away from home, but just took the children off for short day-trips—to the coast and to areas surrounding the village, going off on little jaunts, wherever and whenever we felt like it. And it was good. The children enjoyed themselves, and so did we. And all the while the sun shone down, bleaching Kate's hair bright gold in the highlights, and adding to the freckles across Lucy's nose.

Towards the end of my second week we decided to go again to a lake about a mile from the house. Once a clay pit—though long since disused—the lake was a favourite picnic spot with us, and also an ideal retreat where the children could run and climb to their hearts' content—they had sufficient room for this in our own garden and orchard, but for them, of course, homeground just wasn't exciting enough.

It wouldn't hurt us to walk there, Kate said, so we left the car behind and set off, straggling down the lane in an untidy group —Davie, Lucy and I, then Sam, and then Kate pushing Matthew in his old pram. We had left the late-breakfast dishes soaking in the sink—what Kate called getting one's priorities right.

At the end of the lane Sam threw his ball into the hedge, and as I struggled with the brambles Kate and Lucy went on ahead. By the time I had retrieved it they were some distance away, and we had to hurry to catch them up. When I called out to them to wait they pretended—much to the boys' delight—to treat us as though we were absolute strangers. Kate's face took on the most hammy haughty expression as she turned round to glare at us, sending Lucy into peals of laughter and getting loud chuckles from Davie and Sam.

"Who on earth are those awfully rough people?" Kate asked in a voice not her own. She sounded like some comic dowager, her tone rising and falling a complete octave within the space of words. "I hope they're not going to *bother* us!" And she hurried on, her hips swinging in exaggerated style, while beside her Lucy giggled, unable to contribute more than a token "Humph" before collapsing into laughter.

Kate looked so absurdly young, I thought, watching as she swung away. Her fair hair, straight but curling up at the ends, bounced on her shoulders. Her figure looked so slim, and yet so femininely rounded. I wanted to rush up, put my arms about her waist and kiss the back of her neck where her hair fell parted. But instead I contented myself with a couple of loud comments about the "strange-looking woman up ahead," setting the boys off in chorus with me. And so we made our way to the lake.

We saw the girl sitting on the trunk of a fallen tree, silent, looking out across the water. Her figure was large, swollen with her unborn child. Her hands lay peaceful on the swell of her stomach, her eyes cool, unmoving. She seemed very solitary.

After the first glance neither Kate nor I would have taken any more notice of her—had it not been for Sam. Sam, friendly Sam, went to her, holding out his scraps of bread. He stood there, reaching up, dropping crumbs over her dress and chattering away as he was always ready to do with strangers. Kate gave a theatrical sigh, released a hand from Matthew's pram and beckoned, calling.

"Don't bother the lady. She doesn't want your bits of bread. They're meant for the ducks . . ." Apologetically she smiled, and the young woman smiled back. It was all warmth, openness, all so very ordinary.

Sam went on talking, and in the end Kate went over to him, pushing the pram, with Lucy tagging along. I stayed where I was, waiting for them to rejoin me. But Kate hovered, and I smiled inwardly as I saw her drawn into conversation. It would become Woman's Talk, I was sure, and probably about babies. I couldn't hear their words, only a low murmur that drifted across to me, but I saw the growing impatience in Lucy's sagging pose as she became eager to move on.

Of our four children Lucy, at six, was the eldest. Next to her came Davie—five years old, then Sam who was three, and last of all, Matthew, a mere six weeks. Kate, I know, had been hoping for another girl, but if she *had* felt any disappointment at the birth of a third son she had certainly never shown it.

"Daddy, look at Sam . . ."

Davie was tugging at my hand and pointing to his younger brother. Sam, having wandered off on his own, now stood some distance away at the water's edge, leaning precariously over the bank.

"Be careful!" I yelled, and hurried towards him.

"Watch me!"

Shouting, he proudly tossed his small offerings to the hungry ducks, his unco-ordinated movements almost throwing him off balance. I saw a look of momentary fear on his face as he fought to regain his equilibrium. I grabbed his shirt.

"Yes! You're a clever boy." I swung him off the ground and perched him on my shoulders, his legs straddling my neck. "But you must be careful."

"Why?"

I had no answer for that—*his* stock answer—and let it pass. Davie and Lucy had joined us now, and I turned and looked back to where Kate stood by the fallen tree. Lucy saw my glance and said, "They're gossiping, Daddy. Shall we go on?"

"Yes," I said. "We'll find a good spot to make our camp."

I particularly recall our meandering way around the perimeter of the lake. In some way it seems almost to encapsulate the whole summer—as it was up till that time. Now, still, in my mind's eye I can see Lucy and Sam skirting the water's edge, following in the wake of Davie who walked some yards ahead. They emerge laughing from patches of deep shaded green into warm flowered areas of yellow sunlight. I see them standing dappled by brightness and shadow, patterned by the over-hanging leaves, cupping their hands to their mouths, calling out to each other in their young, enthusiastic voices. I see Davie, his sharp grey eyes following the movements of minnows that dart in the shallows, and hear, still, the cries of delight and surprise: "Look at this!" "Hey, look at that . . ." For them, non-stop explorers, there was no limit to the discoveries to be made.

When at last we came out onto more open ground I called a halt and lounged in the long soft grass. "Let's wait here," I said, stretching out my legs. "Mummy will join us when she's ready. I hope."

Kate was in our view again now. I could see her through the screen of willows. She was sitting by this time. I waved to her but there was no answering gesture: she and the girl were obviously still deep in conversation. I lay back again, closing my eyes against the sun. "She'll find us," I said.

I must have dozed off. I came back to reality at the sound of Kate's voice as she came to us along the footpath. Somebody—it had to be Sam—had taken off my sandals and covered my feet with blades of torn-up grass. I sat up and looked at my watch.

"I haven't been *that* long," Kate said, forestalling any comment I might be about to make.

"Did I say anything?" I asked.

"Come on," she said. "Let's find another spot—with some

room to play. We'll have a game or two and then get lunch."

Magic words. The last bits of grass were brushed from my feet and we moved on. Looking across the lake I saw the girl wave to us as she sat watching our progress. Like well-rehearsed actors we all waved back.

"Have her join us if you'd like to," I said.

"Oh, no, no," Kate said. "We're all right as we are."

Between us we chose a large grassy bank back from the water and partly shaded by the leaves of an oak. Being a weekday, the lake area was fairly quiet. We could be sure of relative seclusion —no footballs thudding into our backs or transistor radios pounding in our ears. I spread out a large tartan blanket on the grass, and Kate sat down on it with Matthew in her arms. He was hungry, and after a quick look to ensure that there were no strangers about, she undid the buttons of her faded denim shirt and let him feed. I watched them. I loved the simplicity of it. I loved her totally unselfconscious acceptance of her role. Behind us in the thicket the others played, unconcerned. The little scene held no interest for them, they had seen it all before.

"Why are you smiling?" Kate asked me, looking up and meeting my eyes.

"You," I said. "You look so pretty."

"Oh, yes, I'm sure." As if to lend absurdity to my remark, she pulled a face, picked a yellow flower from the grass near her feet and put it into her hair. I moved across the intervening space between us and kissed her.

"You okay?" I asked.

"Yes, I'm okay."

She gave me a warm, close smile. Between our bodies Matthew, replete, fell asleep, impervious to everything around him, quite undisturbed by the children's shouts and squeals that rang through the trees and bounced off the water. A dragon-fly darted, hovered and darted, close to the bank. Flies hummed in the warm air. The flower in Kate's hair slipped, tilted, and I reached up and secured it. I kissed her again, lightly. Now, I thought, now—just as it is; I wanted nothing to change.

"Are you happy?" I said.

"What a question." She was doing up the buttons on her shirt.

"Tell me."

"With all I've got," she said, "who wouldn't be."

Later, as I built a fire for the cooking of the sausages, I said: "Did you have a good natter?"

"Mmm?"

"That young woman. By the lake."

"Oh, her . . ." Kate frowned. "She was . . . funny."

"Funny?"

"Not funny . . . just . . . strange. There was something— odd about her . . ."

"How do you mean?"

She paused, considering her words. "Sad. There's something —sad—about her. Different in some way." She shook her head. "It's hard to explain. I don't know . . ."

"Sad . . ."

"Yes."

I sat back on my heels. "It couldn't just be you, could it? With your soft heart for strays . . ."

"That's exactly what she's like," she said quickly. "A kind of —stray person. Almost as if she doesn't really belong."

"She looked perfectly ordinary to me," I said. "What did you talk about?"

"Oh . . . this and that."

"Babies, I expect."

"No." She shook her head. "She didn't seem interested in babies—or any talk of them . . . And yet it appears she's had a number of children . . ."

"More than us?"

"So it seems. And I'll bet she can't be more than in her late twenties." She broke off to call out to the children not to go *too* far away, then turned back to me. "She never mentioned her husband. And going by what little she told me, I gathered that none of her children lives with her."

"You might have got it all wrong," I said. "Perhaps they've all been adopted or something."

She nodded. "Yes, perhaps. Still, there was *something* about her."

The fire had caught now, the flames crackling, devouring the twigs. Through the smoke I looked up across the lake. The girl was still sitting there. I turned my attention away from her, back to the fire, feeding it with the dead wood the children had collected. Kate had put Matthew back in his pram, and now she unpacked the picnic bags—we didn't go in for hampers. She paused in the act of unwrapping the food and straightened up.

"Yes," she said softly, "that's what was particularly weird—the way she held Matthew."

I looked over to where his pram stood in the shade of the leaves. "What do you mean?" I asked. But before she could answer, Davie's voice came ringing out as he bounded, chanting, across the grass towards us, Lucy and Sam following behind and taking up his cry:

"Sausages! Sausages! Who wants sausages!"

And then it was time to eat.

*   *   *

A long time after, when all the food was gone, when the thermoses and the pop bottles were empty and all the games had been played, we packed up to go. At a leisurely pace we moved back around the lake, Sam and Davie on either side of me while Kate and Lucy came close behind with the pram. Lucy, taking the idea from Kate, had picked more flowers, and now the hair of both of them was bedecked with the yellow rockroses, moon daisies and clover.

"I'll tell you what, Daddy . . ." This was Sam, tugging at my left hand, eager to whisper.

I stooped. "Tell me."

"You could be Cyril."

"Who's Cyril?"

"Cyril's the horse. In his book." Davie spoke as if I were a fool not to have known.

I nodded. It was good to know these things. "And what would I have to do?"

"I could ride you to the shop. And we could have ice-cream." Sam again.

"Does Cyril eat ice-cream?"

"I don't know. Big Man does."

"You're Big Man, I suppose."

"Yes."

I hoisted him onto my shoulders as before and he gently prodded me with imaginary spurs while I gripped his ankles.

"Off we go!" he shouted, and we galloped off.

As we ran past the tree-trunk I saw that the young woman had gone. Then, too, she was gone from my thoughts, and Sam and I emerged onto the road where I slowed to a dignified walk.

When Kate, Lucy and Davie caught us up we were standing outside the corner shop eating strawberry and vanilla ice-cream. I went back into the shop and bought more.

"You shouldn't," Kate admonished as I handed her a large cone. She watched for a moment as Lucy ran a pink tongue over the deeper pink of a raspberry ice. "They won't want their supper."

"It's not every day."

Kate nodded. "You've got an answer for everything."

We continued on our way homeward. Sam was on my shoulders again, flagging a little, I knew, after his long day. His hands gripped my hair ("Not too tight there.") while I held tight to his left ankle. Lucy walked at my side and put a small moist hand into my large protective one. I looked down at the crown of her head, onto her straight chestnut hair trimmed with flowers, and as if obeying some secret sign she lifted her chin and gave me a bright smile, her brown eyes shining. I grinned back, winked.

"Tired, chicken?"

"No, not a bit!" She gave a hop, a skip and a jump to prove her point, and a moon daisy flopped, dangled, and fell onto the pavement. She retrieved it and stuck it back behind her ear. "I could stay up forever! And I *will* want my supper!"

*   *   *

As I tucked the sheet up under her chin a couple of hours later she was sound asleep. I thought of her defiant cry and, stooping, lightly kissed her. She stirred for a moment, her mouth tightening from its sleeping slackness, then relaxed again, all softness and vulnerability. I brushed a wisp of hair back from her forehead and murmured into her ear, "Goodnight, chicken licken." For a second I wanted her awake again, resenting, just briefly, her unawareness of my caring. Too soon, I thought, she, like the boys after her, must grow up and grow away from me.

In the next bed Sam sucked his thumb as he slept. And so what? I said to myself. His hair was like Lucy's—straight as a yard of pump water, thick, rich in colour, coarse textured like my own. Beside him, head burrowing into the pillow, Davie lay, hair a shade lighter, and of a finer texture—more like Kate's. On his bedside table was a little mound of stones he had collected. The room was full of his trophies—his maps, the pheasant's feather above the bed. Davie, our incipient naturalist, explorer, botanist, philosopher—you name it. "If you knew the dreams I've got for you," I murmured. I felt sentimental, and so aware of the reality of my happiness.

I sat down on the foot of the bed, looking at the boys' smooth, sunflushed, untroubled faces. There was such a sense of peace there: I must hang on to it while it lasted—as it must surely change—nothing stayed the same . . . Behind me I heard the sound of Kate's soft footsteps as she approached from the doorway. Her hand touched my neck, cool, familiar.

"You really are a hopeless individual." Her voice was low in the quiet.

"Really?"

"Really. It's a damn good job I'm here. They'd be spoilt rotten left to you."

"You're probably right."

"I *know* I'm right . . . And you're quite unashamed."

"*Quite* unashamed." I paused. "But I don't care."

"Good," she said. "I don't either." She stood looking at me for a few seconds, her face shadowy in the dim light. "What were you doing up here so long?"

I shrugged.

"Counting your blessings?" I could just see her smile.

"Something like that," I said. I stood up and put my arms around her. Her hair still smelt of the flowers from the afternoon. It fell soft to her shoulders. I put my face to it, kissed her forehead. Sometimes I still couldn't believe my luck. I felt the softness of her lips against the roughness of my seven o'clock shadow.

"Come on," she whispered after a moment. "Your baby son is waiting downstairs. Waiting to be fed. And he won't be patient much longer."

I was reminded of the pregnant woman by the lake. I said: "What did you mean about that girl . . . ? Something to do with Matthew . . ."

She frowned, thinking back on the afternoon.

"I was rocking Matthew in my arms, and I suggested that she might like to hold him for a while . . ."

"And . . . ?"

"Yes, well, I could tell that she really didn't *want* to. Not really. And when she *was* holding him she made me—nervous."

"I don't get you . . ."

"Well—I don't know—she just held him as if she'd never held a baby before."

"That can't be," I said, "not when she's had several of her own."

"It's true," she said quickly. "Can you remember the day when Lucy was born?—the first time you held her in your arms? You had no confidence at all. Well, she was just like you. So—uncertain. As if the act was quite foreign to her."

From downstairs Matthew's loud yell told us that his hunger was stronger than his patience. I grinned at Kate and she moved towards the landing, but still immersed in her thoughts of the other woman.

"Exactly as if she'd never held a baby before," she murmured. "She didn't know *how* to hold him."

TWO

On Monday, feeling refreshed after my break, I went back to my pictures.

Along with the house, my father had left me a fairly large cottage, and it was there where I worked at my book illustrations. My studio—we always referred to it as "the loft"—occupied the first floor; the ground floor I had converted into a flat and let to a pleasant, elderly couple from London who had come to escape the stairs, hassle and the noise of their city home.

From my windows in the south wall I looked out over the Somerset hills. The other side gave me a view of quiet streets. It was ideal, and situated on the other side of the village from our house, the short mile between the two places gave me the perfect sense of separation of home and work.

I had not always worked in the loft. Before my marriage, and for some time after, I had worked in the house. But as our family grew in size it became more and more apparent that I must find another spot in which to earn our daily bread. Not only because of the growing shortage of space, but also because of the constant, minor interruptions from the children which made concentration increasingly difficult. Sam's arrival clinched it, and when my young school-teacher tenant left the cottage for foreign parts it was the natural choice.

Now I had a quiet place, a place where I could be undisturbed and where, when my working day was over, I could leave everything behind me until the next day.

Also, before, in the house, the lines where work ended and leisure began had become diffused. I could find myself tempted to leave my drawing-board and join Kate or one of the children in their own pursuits. Then come the end of the day, I would berate myself for the unproductive hours. Or, as easily, I might slip into my work-room during the evening—"just for a few minutes"—and realise later that I had been there for hours . . .

It was easier now. I started at a set time, and usually finished at a set time. Office hours, almost, except that my work was more interesting and absorbing than I could ever imagine any office work to be.

At the moment I was working on a rather luxurious new edition of *The Arabian Nights*. It was an interesting assignment and I worked steadily—with a short break for lunch—throughout the day. I was absorbed, totally, in the task before me and was barely aware of the stream of talk and music spewed out by the radio on the shelf above my head. Although I could not tolerate the disturbing sounds imposed on me by other people's radios and other people's chatter I found it easy to work with the sounds of my own choosing, and over which I had complete control—in this case the on/off switch. Sometimes, when I tired of the radio I would play records, putting perhaps the discs of a complete opera on the auto-changer. How much I heard of it would ultimately depend on how engrossed I was in a particular job.

Today I was. During the afternoon I played all of *Lucia Di Lammermoor* and didn't register a single top C.

When, eventually, I looked at my watch I saw with surprise that it was almost six. I had worked way past my usual time. I washed my brushes, put the caps back on the tubes and jars of paint, covered up my unfinished picture and locked the door behind me. Enough was enough for one day.

I reckoned that I must know just about everybody who lived in the village, and as I walked home along the narrow pavements I delighted in the friendly nods and smiles that greeted me from the passers-by. I was aware—viewing it objectively—that I was well-liked, and it gave me a feeling of warm contentment, a sense of belonging. I did belong. I had been born there, and I had grown up there, and every house, every wall, every tree was as familiar to me as the faces of Kate and the children.

Each dwelling I passed I could identify with particular individuals, and I pictured them there behind the screening walls going about their lives: I could almost hear the newspapers rustling, see the meals being prepared, smell the food. Little

Haverstraw was a part of me, and I was part of *it*. I couldn't envisage living anywhere else.

Reaching the end of the main road I turned off up a narrower way into the lane that led to our own house, the grey stone of its walls rising up on the brow of the little hill. This was the view I knew best—as I approached it from the lane—and I loved the look of it through all the seasons. Now I saw in patterned gaps—formed by the vivid green of the hazel and beech trees—the flash of the sun reflecting on the windows, blotting out for a moment the rust-coloured curtains that Kate had hung there.

It was not such a large house. But it was big enough for Kate and me and our growing brood. Standing secluded in its own acre of ground, its situation marked the northernmost point of the village. Our nearest town was some ten or so miles away. For many people, I knew, our lives there, away from the main stream, must appear cut off and insulated. Okay. For me it was fine. It had suited me for all my thirty-seven-odd years and I had no doubt it would continue to do so.

I had brought Kate—a city girl—to the village with certain misgivings after our marriage, concerned lest she would find the pace of life too slow after London, the peace and quiet too much for her city-tuned ears. I need not have worried. She adapted so quickly to country life and never showed any yearning for the more sophisticated existence she had known before. And she was liked by the villagers too—after the first few wary weeks during which they had eyed her, and listened to her London accent with the suspicion they afforded all strangers. But their wariness hadn't lasted long, and in no time at all she had come to be regarded as one of them. As testimony to their affection they took us completely by surprise and clubbed-together to buy for her—on the occasion of Lucy's birth—a beautiful porcelain madonna that she had seen and coveted in a nearby antique shop. She was absolutely overwhelmed by the gesture, and I loved them for it.

Yes, she was happy, and when I did sometimes ask whether she missed her life in London she would treat my question as if it were the height of absurdity: "Sometimes I despair of you."

Now, turning the bend in the lane with the house full in view, Sam came running from the gravel drive and launched himself at me, throwing his arms around my neck.

"The lady's in there!"

"What lady?"

"The *lady*. *You* know. *That* lady."

When we entered the house a minute later I saw that "that lady" was the girl from the lakeside.

* * *

"She's been here for *ages*."

Kate whispered the words to me as I stood in the kitchen pouring an orange squash for our visitor. "No alcohol for me— not in my condition," the girl had said in answer to my offer of a drink. I added American ginger to Kate's scotch and stirred the ice a couple of times. Behind us at the kitchen table the children sat finishing their supper. Soon it would be time for them to be washed and put to bed.

"What's she here for?" I asked.

"God knows. She just turned up on the doorstep. Said someone in the village showed her the way."

On my arrival half-an-hour before I had found the young woman sitting, apparently quite at ease, on the sofa before the empty, open fireplace. One might have supposed that seeing me return from a hard day's work she would consider it the right time to make her departure. Not so. She merely smiled, raising her arm for the brief contact of a handshake:— "Hello, I'm Jane"—then settled comfortably back again. I had not minded; I thought that her presence there might make a welcome change for Kate—we had few visitors.

The girl appeared even younger than in my memory of her. I didn't think she could be more than twenty-six. She had a relaxed, carefree air about her, an unruffleable quality, an air of acceptance of things that made me feel she could be an easy person to know. And yet somehow these very qualities seemed in a way at variance with the youthfulness of her appearance. For a moment I wondered on Kate's earlier comment—that there was something odd about her . . .

I picked up the drinks tray and asked Kate what we should do.

"I don't know," she said. "What *can* we do? Can't very well ask her to go." She sighed. "I've got the children to see to . . ."

I nodded. "I suppose we'll have to ask her to stay for dinner."

"I suppose so. *We've* got to eat sometime. And *you* must be starving."

"To put it mildly."

"Well—" Kate shrugged. "We'll manage somehow." Though I could see she wasn't happy about it. She indicated the tray in my hands. "You'd better take that in. We can't stay out here too long. I'll be in in a moment." Then she turned and gave her attention to Sam who was asking for more pudding.

The girl accepted happily our casual invitation to stay on for "whatever we are having," and sat sipping her orange squash with as much ease as if she lived there.

Later, with the children safely in bed and Matthew settled until the time of his next feed, Kate went back into the kitchen to finish preparing dinner, leaving me and the girl alone. I sat across from her in my easy chair, sipping at my second scotch, the smoke from my cigarette drifting up between us. She had refused a cigarette with the same reason she had given for her refusal of any alcohol. I didn't press her: I admired her willpower.

As the occasional chink of metal and china came from the kitchen—Kate going about her work—the girl asked me about our life in Little Haverstraw and about my occupation there. And I found myself warming to her—perhaps I was flattered by her interest—but she was a good listener and obviously intelligent. She was beautiful too, in a rather wild, undisciplined way. Her blue, blue eyes were steady on my face as I talked and her wide, warm smile made it easy to continue.

When I had finished my cigarette I set the table at the other end of the room. Then the three of us sat down before our plates and Kate served the casserole to which she had added a few more hastily-prepared vegetables.

Over the meal the talk was mostly of generalities and things that affected Kate, me and the family, though I could tell that Kate was trying, in a subtle way, to elicit from the girl some more information about herself. It was only later that I came to realise how unsuccessful she was. By the time the coffee was poured we knew little more about her than we had at the beginning of the evening. We already knew she had had a number of children, but how many, and where they were or what had happened to them we weren't to learn. Neither did she give a hint as to any lover or husband hovering in the background. Whenever she did impart some item relating to her life it was never specific, and any line of conversation that threatened to invade her privacy was deftly dodged and steered back in our direction so that we would find ourselves once again talking of our own lives. The few facts—if you could call them facts—that we *did* manage to glean only served to make her more of a mystery.

After coffee I cleared away the dishes, put them in the sink, and returned to the living-room. The clock on the mantelpiece was striking ten-thirty, but still the girl gave no sign of moving.

As I sat down Kate asked her which part of England she was from.

"How are you so certain I'm from England?" The countering question was accompanied by a little smile.

"Aren't you?" I asked.

"Sometimes. But not always." She paused. "I quite like the summers. Not the winters, though. I hate the cold weather. My God, I could never stand an English winter, I'm *sure!* I always have to get going."

"Get going?" Kate echoed. "Where? What do you mean?"

"Oh . . ." A shrug, another smile. "I follow the sun. It's the only thing to do."

Our conversation became more and more desultory. I took another surreptitious look at the clock and saw that the hands now marked ten-past eleven. We plodded on.

And then, at eleven-forty-five, the girl showed signs of moving. She rose awkwardly from the sofa and Kate and I exchanged flickering, thankful glances—at last our visitor was going. But she merely asked where the bathroom was, and then stood aside while Kate preceded her into the hall to show the way.

When Kate returned alone a moment later she raised her eyes to the ceiling in despair. I grinned at her.

"That'll teach you to get into conversation with strange women."

"My God. Will she *never* go?" She was keeping her voice low. "I've never met anyone *like* her! Surely she's not expecting us to invite her to stay the night."

"No, don't worry," I said. "She'll leave soon. She *must*. Anyway, I can't stay up too late—I've got a lot of work to get through tomorrow."

"So have I."

I could see the tiredness in Kate's face. The evening had proved a strain, and with Matthew at the age he was we had as yet no certainty that he would sleep the night through and not waken in the small hours demanding to be fed.

"She'll probably leave when she comes out of the loo," I said.

"God, I hope so."

She gave a loud yawn, then attempted to stifle it as the stranger came back into the room, smiling as she came towards us. Almost in disbelief I watched as, with a sigh of contentment, the girl once again settled herself down on the sofa.

It was after twelve-thirty when she at last got up to go.

With such a feeling of relief I went into the hall and collected her coat. I could hardly believe she was finally on her way. Though I would probably have to drive her, I supposed: we could scarcely let her walk home alone, and it was obvious that she had no other means of transport.

"I've been the most dreadful nuisance, I know," she said as I helped her on with her coat. And both Kate and I protested—almost in chorus—saying what a nice surprise her visit had been, and how much we had enjoyed it. Later, I told myself, we would berate each other for the hypocrites we were.

As we followed her to the front door I insisted—getting deeper into the Good Host role—that I run her home in the car. She shook her head adamantly.

"No. No, indeed not. I wouldn't hear of it. I'll walk." She pointed vaguely off into the night in the direction of the open fields. "It's not far."

"But I must," I said. "It's the least I can do."

"No. Really, thank you, but I'll be all right."

She was still standing in the open doorway, all ready to go, and still not going.

"It's a lovely night," she said, gazing up at the star-dotted sky. "I love nights like this."

Kate, at my shoulder, gave me a look as if asking whether we were in for a conversation about the weather. I nodded, then said to the girl: "I insist. Really," and went to step by her to lead the way.

And all at once she was clutching at me, her nails digging into my arm, her mouth twisted slightly in a little grimace of pain. For a moment I just stared at her, nonplussed, then I looked over her head into Kate's surprised eyes. Kate said quickly: "Get her into the spare room."

The spare room—once my studio and now more of a junk room than anything else—had a bed in it, and between us Kate and I managed to get her along the passage towards it. And all the time the girl's body was wracked by quickening spasms, her breath coming in painful gasps.

"Call an ambulance," Kate said. I had laid the girl on the bed and now stood helplessly gazing down at her.

"Go on!" Kate said, and I hurried back into the living-room, her voice calling after me to hurry.

Two minutes later I was back at her side. She looked at me with a flash of desperation in her eyes.

"Did you get through all right?"

"The phone's out of order."

"Nonsense! It was okay earlier today."

"I can't help that," I said. "It's as dead as hell right now."

"Try again."

"There's no point in it," I said. "It's dead."

On the bed at our side the girl gave another cry, hands to her belly, her back arching.

"Well, we can't stand here discussing it," Kate said. "You'll have to go and get Doctor Collins. Get him to come out."

I nodded, took my keys from my pocket, and ran out to the garage.

The doctor was in. He was in bed. His wife answered the door, looking elegant in her dressing-gown, and unable to quite restrain a faint look of annoyance that he should be disturbed. This was his night off, she said, and they hadn't long returned from a dinner-party in Axbridge. Then she summoned a smile and turned away and I waited, fretting on the doorstep, while she went to fetch him. He came down the stairs some minutes later, a square, muscular little man whose ruddy complexion and tweed jacket gave him more the appearance of a farmer than anything else. He gave a quick look at the anxiety in my face and said simply, "Give me a moment to get my bag and I'll be right with you."

Soon after, his new dark-blue Vauxhall was following my old light-grey Ford out of the drive and onto the road.

From the time of my leaving to the time of my return it had only been about twenty minutes. But it was enough. By that time it was all over.

With Collins right behind me I entered the room to find it in turmoil. Jugs, kettles and a large plastic water-filled bowl stood on the floor near my feet, while all around were strewn towels and articles of clothing. On the narrow bed the girl lay sleeping, the blankets drawn up to her chin. At her side in a wicker chair sat Kate, the new-born baby in her arms.

THREE

Holding a finger to her lips, she urged me not to make any noise. She whispered, smiling: "It's the dearest little girl . . ."

Kate's brow was damp with sweat, I noticed. Her face was flushed, and the fabric of her blouse was darkened beneath the armpits. But she looked very calm. Gently she pulled back the shawl—one of Matthew's—to allow us to see the infant.

"Isn't she a picture . . . ?"

She was.

I gazed down at a perfect little face.

The tiny baby had nothing of that pinched, angry look with which so many new-born babies face the world. Against the white shawl her cheeks were softly smooth and glowing, framed by fine, pale-blonde curls. Her eyes, shut tight in sleep, were fringed with thick, dark lashes.

"She's lovely," I said, then watched as the doctor took her into his arms.

"Why don't you go and relax?" he asked me.

"I'm not the one who's done the work," I said. But I nodded, grinned briefly at Kate—a very proud Kate—and left them to it.

In the living-room I sat in my arm-chair and lit a cigarette. On an impulse I lifted the telephone receiver and listened for the dial tone. Still nothing. And then I saw that the cord had come adrift from the wall-socket. How could it have happened? Had I done it when shifting the chair earlier in the evening? Surely I'd have been aware: it would take more than a little effort to rip one of those things out . . .

After a few minutes Kate came in, the baby once again close in her arms. Behind her came the doctor.

"She'll be fine," he announced, jerking his head back in the direction of the spare room. "Your wife did an excellent job." He gave Kate a congratulatory smile.

"I can't take much credit," Kate said. "It was all so easy. Surprisingly so. And so quick. I hardly had to do anything."

With each one of our own children Kate had had a relatively difficult time. Now she still seemed surprised that the child she held could have been born without the struggle and the pain she had experienced herself.

"It was over almost before I knew it," she said. "And anyway, she—Jane—seemed to know exactly what to do . . ."

A little later I wheeled in Matthew's pram and Kate placed the new baby in it. Collins watched her, then picked up his bag. There was nothing more he could do for the present.

"I've made out the birth-certificate." He was moving towards the door. "I left it on the side table. I'll look in again tomorrow."

"Shouldn't she—er—the mother—go to a hospital or something . . . ?" I asked.

He hesitated, hand on the door-latch.

"Well, there's no *need* for it. I mean, she's perfectly fit. Strong as an ox, in fact. Of course, I could get her to one if you insist, though I'm sure she'd be much happier staying here for a couple of days—if you could manage it . . ." His suggestion hung in the air.

Kate looked questioningly over at me. I could do nothing but agree.

"Of course," I said.

When he had left, Kate looked in at the girl and saw that she was still sleeping. I made some tea, and then together the two of us sat down, glad of the chance to relax again. The house was very still, taking on that special kind of quiet which is peculiar to the small hours. I was aware of the creaks in the timbers as they settled for the night, the ticking of the clock.

But the silence didn't last long. Suddenly, from upstairs, came Matthew's full-throated yell. Kate got quickly to her feet.

"My God. With all the excitement I forgot his last feed!" And she hurried from the room.

A couple of minutes later his cries had stopped. I smiled to myself. He was obviously getting what he wanted.

I poured another cup of tea and continued to sit there. When Kate returned she said: "He's gone off again okay," and moved over to the pram to peer down at the baby girl.

"Look at her," she said. "She's really such a dear little thing."

The baby's mother awoke soon afterwards, and I made fresh tea and followed Kate as she wheeled the pram from the living room.

We found the girl sitting up against the pillows lighting a cigarette. She smiled at us.

"I can smoke now. Now it's safe."

Kate manoeuvred the pram into the room and parked it a couple of feet from the bed. The girl gave it a glance and then turned her eyes to me, giving me a grateful nod as I handed her the cup.

"I really am such a bother. All this trouble I'm putting you to. You'll think twice before you befriend another pregnant woman."

Kate sat on the edge of the bed and admonished her gently. "Now you stop that. Thank God we were able to help. Just think, if you'd left five minutes earlier—and *walked* as you insisted—you'd be lying in a ditch somewhere. *Then* what would you have done?"

"Oh, dear, what a terrible thought."

Kate studied her as she drew on her cigarette. She said: "Aren't you curious?"

"What about?"

"Well—" Kate seemed almost at a loss. "Well, about *her*. Your little girl." She nodded towards the pram. "You haven't really seen her yet."

"Oh. Oh, yes . . . Yes, of course." The girl replaced the cup on the side-table, took one last drag on her cigarette, and stubbed it out. Kate rose, took the still-sleeping baby from the pram and placed her in the mother's arms. The girl looked down at the child dispassionately.

"Seems such a shame to disturb her," she said.

As I watched her holding the baby I remembered Kate's words when she had spoken of the way the girl had held Matthew: "As if the act was quite foreign to her." I could see what she had meant.

The girl held her baby in a cool, detached way. And when

she looked at it—which was just the briefest glance—her eyes were quite devoid of any motherly devotion. There was absolutely no thrill in the contact, you could see.

I thought at first that it must be my imagination, but then I saw that Kate was as aware as I was. She looked on helplessly for a moment then said, with a touch too much eagerness,

"I fed her. I gave her a bottle. I hope you don't mind, but she was hungry, and I didn't want to wake you."

No concern showed in the girl's face. "Good," she said. "I expect she would be. Thank you."

There was a short pause. Kate said lamely:

"I didn't know what to do for the best . . ."

There was no answer. She shrugged. "Perhaps I should have awakened you. I mean, I don't know what your plans are. You probably intend to breast-feed her . . . I do with Matthew. I have with all our children . . ."

"Oh, God, no." The girl gave a short shake of her head as if the idea was abhorrent to her. "I've never done anything like that, and I can't see myself starting now."

She continued to hold the baby in that stiff, awkward, unfeeling way, and I could see that Kate was becoming more and more agitated. Then lifting up the baby in her arms, the girl said matter-of-factly:

"I'm sure she'd be more comfortable in the pram."

Kate moved almost too quickly. As she took the child she breathed the faintest sigh of relief. The girl heard it and said apologetically:

"It's just that I'm so tired . . ."

"Oh, of *course* you are," Kate said. There was contrition in her voice.

"And I've got a long way to go tomorrow." The girl frowned. She looked more than a little worried. I cut in quickly:

"Don't you think about that. I'll take you home when you're ready to go. There's no hurry. Just relax. Don't worry about a thing."

"You're so kind to me. Both of you."

Somehow, nothing seemed quite right. And now the rich

sound of sincerity in her voice jarred with the oddness of the situation. There was an awkward silence suddenly, then Kate said:

"I'll put her back in the pram, shall I? She'll be all right there for the night."

"Oh, yes, that'll be fine. Thank you. I'm sure she'll be perfectly comfortable."

When the baby was settled Kate went out to the kitchen and returned a few minutes later with a feeding bottle, a thermos and some powdered milk.

"Look," she said, "this is for her next feed. All you've got to do is mix it and give it to her—" She broke off, smiling. "Listen to me, telling you what to do. As if you didn't know perfectly well."

The girl smiled, picked up her cup and sipped at her tea. Kate watched her for a second or two then said, "You must be very, very proud of her, I'm sure." She wasn't at all sure, I knew.

"Oh, dear, I'm so tired." The girl was yawning. "And you two must be exhausted."

I *was* tired now. "Yes, I am a little," I said. I had already decided to forgo part of my work the following day. I moved towards the door, Kate at my side.

"All right then?" Kate asked, turning in the doorway.

"Yes, thank you." The girl stubbed out her cigarette and lit another. "Just one last cigarette and then I'll get off to sleep." She looked at our faces and gave a small laugh. "Don't worry, I won't set the place on fire."

We said our goodnights. Just before I closed the door she said:

"Thank you again. I'm more grateful than you can imagine."

*   *   *

Upstairs in our bedroom I emerged from the bathroom to find Kate sitting up in bed with a preoccupied frown on her face.

"What's up?" I asked.

"Everything." She shook her head. "That poor baby . . ."

"Now don't you start worrying," I said. "There's nothing we can do."

"But it's so *unfair!* What kind of a life is she going to have—with such a mother! She doesn't care *that* much for her! It's criminal!"

"Well, maybe it's not as bad as it looks."

She ignored this. "That lovely, lovely child," she said. "How can that girl be so unfeeling."

"Don't worry about it. Don't think about it."

I switched off the light, moved to the window and drew back the curtains. Moonlight filtered into the room, very bright, casting a shadow of leaves on the carpet and the pale-blue bedspread. I could plainly see Matthew asleep in his cot. I went to him, leaning down, heard his gentle, regular breathing.

"Nothing bothers him," I said.

"No . . ." Now I could hear a smile in Kate's voice. I sat down on the edge of the bed, reached out, touched her shoulder. "You're too sensitive."

"No. Not too sensitive," she answered. "Just normal, I hope."

A little later, just as I was drifting off, she murmured into my ear:

"Don't forget, we must call the GPO in the morning—get the telephone repaired."

"Okay," I said. I wanted to sleep.

"What was wrong with it?"

"I think *I* did it." I could hear my voice slurred. "When I moved the chair earlier on. Must have been. The cord got ripped out of its socket . . ."

Her hand came around me and pressed on my chest.

"You big brute," she said.

*   *   *

It was only a few hours later when Matthew woke us yelling for his early-morning feed. As we surfaced, sleepily, we became aware also of the crying of the infant downstairs. Her squalling rang through the house.

"My God, she's got a good pair of lungs," Kate said, smiling.

Gathering Matthew into her arms she brought him back to the bed where he hungrily latched on to her breast. "You go on back to sleep," she told me. "I shall join you just as soon as this one's finished with me." I yawned, nodded, and turned over on my side again.

I didn't get back to sleep that morning. And neither did Kate. Long after Matthew had been fed and changed and safely bedded down again in his cot, the baby downstairs was still crying. Kate fought against the noise for some time, then sat up in bed.

"Whatever is that woman doing? Isn't she looking after it, or what?" She listened, frowning, hugging her knees and poised for action while I watched from sleepy, half-closed eyes. Then she got out of bed and reached for her dressing-gown, her voice growing angry.

"I can't stand that. I can't just lie here and listen to that baby crying its head off. Whatever can the woman be thinking of!"

As she hurried from the room a glance at the bedside clock told me it was just after seven-thirty.

The next moment, over the sound of the baby's cries, Kate's voice came, calling my name. I rose in a panic and hurried down to her. She was standing in the doorway of the spare room, an anxious, puzzled look on her face.

"What's happening?" I asked.

"What's *happening*? You tell me. I wish I knew." She turned and waved a hand at the room's interior. "I don't understand anything."

In the pram the baby lay bawling at the top of her lungs. She had kicked the covers away from her body and now lay exposed to the cool morning air. Beside her, untouched, was the water and the powdered milk that Kate had left. The bed where the girl had lain was untidy and empty. Of the girl herself there was no sign.

FOUR

"How did it go today?"

Kate's voice came to me from the living-room as I stood in the hall hanging up my jacket.

"Okay," I said. It had. I had completed the last of the *Arabian Nights* illustrations, packed them up and got them off to the publisher.

"Did you finish?"

"Yes. Thank God." I lingered, turfing cigarettes and matches from my pockets. "I was pleased with them. I think they will be too."

When I went into the room I saw her sitting on the sofa with Jane Bryant's baby at her bare breast. I stood there for a moment, just looking. She said:

"Oh, come on, darling. Don't look like that."

"Like what?"

"That—reproving—slightly shocked expression you get sometimes."

"Sorry," I said. "It's just a bit of a surprise, that's all."

She adjusted the baby's position in the crook of her arm. "Well, you must admit it's pretty silly to breast-feed one and mix powdered milk for the other isn't it?"

I said nothing. She prompted me gently.

"Well, isn't it?"

"I suppose so."

"Of course it is, dear."

And of course she was right, I told myself after a little consideration. Thinking of it objectively, I suppose I had felt jealous—seeing the baby girl as some kind of usurper. It was the most natural and beautiful thing to see Kate feeding my own son—but a stranger's child—that was a different matter.

Kate said gently:

"Matthew's losing nothing by it, darling."

"No. . . ."

Matthew lay on the sofa next to her, smiling at nothing in particular, hands reaching up into the air. I noticed the contrast between the pale-gold curls of the baby girl and his own dark wisps. Kate grinned down at him.

"He's all right."

"Oh, yes. . . ."

"It's the least we can do—look after her." Kate sighed and shook her head. "I'll never understand it. How could anyone walk out and abandon such a dear little creature. . . ."

It was a week since the baby's birth and the subsequent disappearance of her mother. We had waited a couple of days thinking she might reappear, but there had been nothing, no sign, no word. It was then that we had contacted the local authorities telling them that the baby had been left with us. The social worker, Miss Jenkins, who came to the house without delay, agreed to Kate's request to let the baby stay with us for a while "until such time as Jane Bryant could be found."

But all attempts to trace her failed. There was so little known about her for anyone to go on, and in the end we just ran out of ideas. The police, in spite of their efforts, met with no success at all, and the only clue to her whereabouts came from a local farmer who, passing through the village that same morning about half-past five, had seen a woman answering her description walking towards the main road. He had described her as "being in a bit of a hurry,"—wherever she was going she was wasting no time. After that the trail stopped. As far as we were concerned she might as well have vanished from the face of the earth.

Now I studied Kate as she sat with the baby in her arms. I heard the voracious sounds coming from the tiny mouth and resentment stirred in me again.

"They've got to find her. She's got to be somewhere. She can't be *that* far away."

Kate said nothing. I added:

"Who knows—she *might still* come back for her."

"Oh, no. She won't come back."

"How can you be so sure?" I was sure myself.

"She won't come back. She has no intention of ever coming back. You know that."

Yes. The woman's behaviour had never given the remotest hint of any maternal feeling. It was quite obvious that she had left the child to its fate. Even so I couldn't give up.

"You never know," I said.

"Are you trying to convince yourself?"

She didn't expect an answer. She smiled down at the baby. "Isn't she a picture? She's such a lovely little thing."

At the words the baby stopped feeding and looked up at her with wide, deep blue eyes, a little smear of milk on her pink, tiny mouth, her face bearing an expression of the deepest trust and love. She reached up and clutched at Kate's forefinger.

"Look at her!" Kate whispered in awe. "She's gripping me so tightly. It's incredible—she's only a week old!"

She lifted the baby higher in her arms, holding her cheek-to-soft-cheek, creating a picture of motherhood that any photographer would have given his eye-teeth to snap.

"Oh, you are a bonnie little girl."

And Bonnie got her name.

*   *   *

Kate seemed to feel compelled to take it upon herself to make up to the baby for the loss of her real mother. As the days passed I watched as she bestowed on the infant a love and protection that was almost fierce in its intensity. Her eventual words came as no real surprise to me.

"We must keep her, Alan. . . ."

There was no hint of a question in her words. Her mind was made up. For her, no other course was open.

"Steady on," I said. "We can't just do that."

"Why not?"

"Well. . . ."

"Why not?" she repeated. "*Someone's* got to look after her. She'll either be put in an orphanage or go to foster-parents. Why shouldn't *we* be her foster-parents."

I kept silent. She went on:

"You know damn-well her mother will never come back. Even the police told us there's very little hope of that. No one knows anything about her. They don't even know where she was living or where she came from. Nobody knows anything."

I turned away. There were all kinds of reasons why we should not embark on the upbringing of another child.

"We've got enough to cope with," I said. "We've got our own children. How would you manage?"

"I'll already be looking after one baby. Looking after another at the same time wouldn't be difficult."

"The cost . . ." I said lamely.

"That's no problem. They don't expect you to rear a foster-child without some financial help. We'd get some little grant or something . . . But we don't need it, *anyway*. We could manage perfectly well as it is." She paused, waiting, watching my face. "You *know* her mother doesn't want her. And besides, she no longer has any *right* to her. She forfeited that right when she walked out and left her to cry. No one—no one at all has a better right to care for her than we do."

*   *   *

Kate had her way.

After various interviews with social workers—when they sat in the house giving us the once-twice-and-thrice-over, assessing us and the suitability of our environment—we became Bonnie's foster-parents. And it was only then that Kate relaxed. The matter was settled—subject, of course, to the satisfactory reports which Miss Jenkins would have to make after her periodic visits to check on Bonnie's welfare.

I could tell then, watching Kate's face, just how much it all meant to her, and I was happy, seeing her happiness, knowing I had done right to agree. Already she seemed to regard the child as her own—so much so, I thought, that *should* Jane Bryant ever return to claim her daughter the resulting confrontation would, to say the least, be traumatic. But I could see no likelihood of such an event ever taking place.

Bonnie was a beautiful baby. She had a voracious appetite for both food and affection and, with her share of each, thrived splendidly. She was so healthy, and she had such happy, endearing ways that it was impossible not to love her. In no time at all she had been accepted as part of the family.

Of course it was necessary to make a few changes. We ditched Matthew's pram—a hand-me-down from Lucy, Davie and Sam—and bought one designed for twins. We bought a new cot, too. From now on Matthew and Bonnie would sleep and ride together.

Late in September Kate and I and our enlarged family made another excursion to the lake. It was different now. The leaves were turning and we had seen the last of the summer. In the shade of the willows the tree-trunk where the girl had sat in her orange frock was bare. We knew she had gone out of our lives for ever.

And we had adapted so readily to the changes she had brought about in our lives. Bonnie's coming had naturally made a difference, but we settled, happily, easily, falling into our newly-established patterns. Kate was happy, the children were happy, and I was happy. What more could we want?

* * *

Early one grey October morning as I stood shaving before the bathroom mirror Kate ran in screaming from the bedroom. She made me jump so violently that I nicked my chin with the razor. A solitary bird had been singing outside the window, and as Kate's cries rang out he took to his wings and flew away. Her voice shrieked, splintering the gentleness of the day, words pouring from her mouth in an incoherent stream. She clutched me, dragging at me so that the towel I had tied around my waist fell to the floor and I stood ridiculously naked in the face of her anguish.

"Quick . . . ! Quick . . . ! Oh, God, *please* . . . !"

With the lather drying on my face I followed her at a rush into the bedroom and over to the babies' cot. Bonnie, awakened by Kate's screaming, had begun to cry, reaching out her arms, asking for comfort.

At the other end of the cot Matthew lay. The strange colour of his face, the coldness of his smooth skin and the stillness of his little body told me he would never move again.

FIVE

For a long time it seemed that we would never be free of the tragedy. For weeks Kate was inconsolable. She mooned about the house with great sad eyes and trying, desperately trying, to be brave and not give way to her feelings in front of the children. They didn't realise what had happened; only Lucy, in some vague, unreal way, was at all aware that there was such a thing as death, and now, in her child's mind, she linked Matthew's passing with that of a kitten she had owned the year before—a small black and white pet that had died after being savaged by a wandering dog.

"Matthew's like Tommy, isn't he, Mummy?"

She asked the question matter-of-factly, looking up from the book she was reading. It was just over a week since the funeral. Kate didn't answer and turned away.

"*Matthew*, Mummy—he's like Tommy, my cat."

"Yes, dear," Kate said wearily. "Like Tommy . . ."

Kate blamed herself. That was one of the hardest things to live with, and no amount of talk from me could shake her from the belief that she was in some way responsible. How? she continually asked. How could she have allowed her child to just suffocate?—to just lie there in his cot and suffocate?—surely she should have been aware of all the dangers, the chances, the risks —the very tenuousness of a baby's hold on life.

Even Doctor Collins, seeing her state of mind, could give her little solace. "These cot-deaths do happen," he told her. "They're not common, but they do happen. It was an accident. You mustn't blame yourself . . ."

Kind words, meant to comfort, but nothing could dispel for Kate her picture of Matthew as she had found him that morning, lying twisted up in his nursery sheet (evidence of his struggle to survive)—his Rupert Bear blanket stretched tight across his transfixed mouth. My own words of reassurance sounded feeble when pitched against her sadness, and I could do little more than attempt to submerge my own feelings of grief.

It was a blessing, I thought—as far as Kate was concerned—that the other children were there. The demanding nature of their presence took up so much of her time and attention that she was left with little time to brood. Before Matthew's death I had urged her for the fiftieth time to think about getting some help around the house, and, just as before, she had said yes, she would think about it—and that was where it always ended. Now, returning home after a day in the loft, and seeing how full had been her own time, I was thankful for her past procrastinations.

Bonnie, being the youngest, was the most demanding of all. No matter how much one might be suffering, still Bonnie had to be fed, changed and bathed. I looked at her as she lay sleeping peacefully in her cot and was so thankful for her—an absolute Godsend, I told myself.

And gradually, as the weeks passed, normality crept back into the atmosphere of the house, though things, I knew, would never be *quite* the same again. It was just that now, normality was a little different. But we adjusted. We got used to it. Slowly the colour came back to Kate's cheeks and she ceased to force the thoughts of Matthew from her mind. As time went by she found she could live with his images; the memories of him became easier to bear.

It is true: Kate was more affected by the loss of Matthew than I was. It was obvious. Speaking for myself, he had not yet become any kind of personality: he was so *very* young. I was deeply saddened by his death, of course, but he had been with us such a short time that his sudden passing made me feel I had never really got to know him. But with Kate it was different. Through the years, as we had grown closer together, I had watched motherhood take its hold on her—and I had adored and respected her for it—but it was only now, seeing her grief, that I came to realise how completely she could love, and just how strong and deeply-rooted her maternal instincts were.

Kate and I had first met some seven-odd years before in London at a party given to launch a series of children's books that I had illustrated. It was a small affair—thirty or forty professional people and friends standing around holding glasses of sherry and filling the air with smoke and the right kind of small talk, and probably—as I was—waiting for a suitable time to pass before making the necessary excuses that would enable one to get the hell out.

I saw Kate across the room as she entered—quite beautiful and rather late—on the arm of an old art-school-friend of mine. Her face seemed vaguely familiar to me and I thought perhaps we must have met before, briefly, at some forgotten moment. When, eventually, we were introduced her name also rang bells and I told her I had been trying to figure out when and where we had previously bumped into each other—not having had much to do with the London scene since my student days, I didn't have much to work with.

"No," she said, "we've never met before. I'd remember."

"I'm sure of it," I protested. "I know your face."

The art-school-friend laughed then, and said it wasn't so surprising since Kate had achieved considerable success in a long-running television serial which had only just ended. And she laughed too, saying she could tell what I didn't do with my evenings.

I felt abashed by my ignorance, and slightly embarrassed, but to her it didn't seem to matter. She seemed amused by the idea that I had managed to live for so long without a television set—although, as I told her, I did "occasionally go to the pictures." I realised then that it was in the odd film and the newspapers where I had probably seen her face.

Knowing next-to-nothing of the world of show-business I would have been interested to learn something about her career, but she steered clear of it, telling me in her low, slightly husky voice that it wasn't nearly as fascinating as people imagined, and that she didn't want to celebrate our meeting by boring me to death. Instead, she asked me questions about myself, saying that she had admired my work for a long time, and had bought several of the books I had illustrated. Tritely I said I hoped her children enjoyed them, to which she replied that she had no children, wasn't married, and had bought the books simply for her own pleasure.

It was at this point that the old art-school-friend saw another old friend over on the far side of the room and politely excused himself. I excused him gladly and gave him a silent blessing for leaving us alone together. I didn't miss his presence.

I had never met anyone like her before and, talking to her, I realised I had always seen actresses in my mind's eye as something from a race apart—women who figured in divorce cases and sensational headlines; self-absorbed, emasculating women who were concerned solely with their own careers and images. And Kate was not like that. She had wide interests and a sense of humour. There was a genuineness about her, a gentle warmth. And with her real modesty and simplicity she was utterly appealing.

I no longer kept glancing at my watch. With *her* standing there I wanted the party to go on, only sorry that the time would come when she would have to leave.

Half an hour later, before she had been commandeered by our returning mutual friend and taken out into the late afternoon I had managed to suggest—in the most tentative, circuitous way imaginable—that I contact her when next I was coming to London.

She nodded, "Okay," and delved into her handbag—a large, cumbrous-looking canvas thing—and produced an old envelope. Adding her telephone number to her name and address, she handed it to me with a smile.

"Here . . . I have these things specially printed. I believe in style."

I folded the envelope and thrust it into my pocket.

"I'll be in touch . . ."

When I got home I took out the envelope and read it.

"Well, Miss Kate Robbins," I said aloud, "I think I shall probably be in London again very soon . . ."

I was.

Two days later I telephoned her saying that I had a business appointment in Holborn and that it would be nice if we could possibly meet—if she was possibly free—and possibly have lunch together, or dinner . . . possibly . . .

I can remember my nervousness as I waited in the Notting Hill Gate restaurant—she suggested which one—for her to join me. Half of me knew that she would not fail to keep the appointment and the other half wondered what she could find to interest her in the company of a parochial, self-sufficient artist from a small Somerset village; someone who didn't even own a television set, only occasionally went to the cinema, and knew nothing at all about her own career or way of life.

And then she was there, coming through the door, seeing me, walking towards me.

She was casually dressed in a wool suit of saxe blue, and the colour reflected in her eyes, changing, deepening the grey that I remembered. Her shoulder-length fair hair swung across her cheek as she sat down. I smiled at her and said fatuously:

"Well—here you are . . ."

"Yes," she said, "here I am . . ."

We lunched—a long, leisurely lunch—and I relaxed and grew happier and happier in her company. I'd never met anyone like her before and I didn't want our time together to come to an end. But of course it had to. She had an appointment at four o'clock at the Television Centre, she told me, and I became unbearably aware of the passing time, the minutes running out and abandoning me. And then, at last, much too soon, they had nearly all gone.

"I shall really have to dash," she said, "or I'll never get there." She glanced again at her watch and then looked across at me. "What about your own appointment? What time is that?"

I'd quite forgotten the excuse I'd given for my visit to London. Now, facing her, various possible elaborations of the lie went flitting through my mind. I rejected them all and in the end said nothing. She said nothing either, but just smiled, warm, knowing the truth.

The waiter brought back my change from the bill and I counted silver onto the plate. I looked up to see her eyes, steady, studying me across the table. She sat very still, as if allowing the progress of some inner debate. Then she said:

"But I'm quite free after my interview . . ."

*   *   *

When we met that evening it was in her Hampstead flat. I sipped a scotch-and-water while she finished getting ready, and then together we went out into the street. "I'm in your hands," I said, and she laughed and told me I mustn't make rash state-ments—that verbal agreements were as binding as written ones.

By mutual agreement we left the car where it was and walked half-a-mile up the hill to a small Italian restaurant where we were greeted by friendly waiters. As we were shown to a table in a fairly secluded corner I was aware of covert glances directed at Kate from one or two of the other diners—either due to the fact that they recognised her or because she just looked so mar-vellous; I didn't care which—I only knew I was glad and proud to be with her.

Sitting opposite, I watched her in the warm glow. She was dressed quite differently now, wearing a soft, light-looking dress in charcoal grey with little patterns of gold at her neck and wrists. Her canvas bag had been switched in favour of a small, black, compact model.

When the wine had been poured she looked at me over the rim of her glass—those grey eyes—and I knew suddenly, just knew, that I had reached a watershed in my life—that the time was coming soon when I would have to make a decision.

I was pushing thirty-one. I had had a couple of short-lived affairs during my studies in London and afterwards fewer-and-further-between flings closer to home (there was far less oppor-tunity there), but I had never treated any of it seriously—not with any view to permanence. Then, living alone after the death of my parents my life had become increasingly insulated as I got more and more wrapped-up in my work. My aloneness hadn't bothered me, though—I wasn't a gregarious person—and I never gave any constructive thought to what might follow. I had, over

the years, I realised, come to accept—without design or consideration—a state of bachelorhood which, on reflection, seemed
well-set to be the pattern for the future.

But Kate changed all that.

I was probably a bit of a fool that night. But the wine—like
the situation—went to my head. I'm sure I smiled too much. I
know I talked too much. But we both did—rambling on about
everything, just cramming the streams of words into the space of
time. And as we talked I became aware of our conversation hiding secret looks and touches. Our fingers brushed, and finally
pressed as we exchanged cigarettes and tasted each other's food.
I put a morsel of chicken into her mouth and then put the fork,
unladen, into my own mouth, watching her watching me, the
warmth, the steadiness in her eyes.

I wanted her very much, and I'm sure that the wanting was
naked in my face and in my voice. How could I have hidden it?
And I flaunted my desire within the circle of light coming from
the candle that burned in the red glass holder between us. Everything was like some huge festive secret, as if our growing
closeness, our happiness, was one-up on the other diners—not
that we noticed them—and as if they could really have cared
less, anyway. And always the conversation going on, almost as if
that alone was the purpose of our being there.

But what sweet luxury to know that a greater sweetness was
in store. And to put that sweetness off—another glass of wine?—
another cup of coffee?—to delay it for the longest possible time—
not from fear, but from wanting; making it even sweeter, knowing it would be mine, as I did know it would be.

In exchange for the piece of chicken she took a bit of garlic
bread and put it to my lips, and I took her thumb, so briefly, into
my mouth along with the bread. I couldn't get close enough.
What did it matter if anyone saw? I couldn't be concerned with
others—not when there was this turmoil of thoughts and feelings, hands brushing, limbs covered by clothing, fingers on
fingers, breath catching on the surprise of deviously arranged
contact. Then the eyes and the looks—and none of it was
enough. Would anything be?—ever?

"You don't know what you're doing to me," I said.

"Am I—doing anything?"

"Correction. You *do* know."

"Perhaps."

And she drank from my wineglass to show that she could do anything.

*   *   *

Later, much later, lying in her bed, I looked out at the stars that showed between the partly-open curtains. She stirred against me in the crook of my arm, her hand light across my chest. I would have to move my position soon, I thought—I could feel my arm growing steadily numb. But not yet. Not while she burrowed so warmly against me like this.

In her sleep she murmured some incoherent, brief word and I left the sky and looked down at her tousled hair. I knew now. I knew, that as far as I was concerned, my decision was made.

That was in March. Just over four weeks later we were married.

SIX

Bonnie was a remarkable child. She crawled long before she was five months old, and Christmas found her scrabbling about the house at a speed that amazed us. Kate would look at her with continuing astonishment, saying that she had never seen anything like it.

Miss Jenkins, calling at the house to check on Bonnie's well-being, was delighted with the progress and contentment she exhibited. "Though," she said, smiling over her cup of tea, "I'm afraid you spoil her."

"Oh, no," Kate said quickly, and then relaxed, seeing there had been no implied criticism in the words. She smiled. "But she's such a darling. Everyone loves her."

It was true. Everyone did. Sam and Davie showed it in their unquestioning acceptance of her presence there—as they would have with any younger brother or sister—their feelings a mixture of tolerance, patience, natural affection, and the consideration that anyone more helpless demanded of them.

With Lucy—perhaps because she was that much older—it was slightly different. She seemed always very much aware that Bonnie had—so fortuitously—*just come to us*—out of the blue, almost. And her delight and surprise that such a wonderful thing could have happened was always there. For all her gentleness, she was fiercely protective, and very loving and loyal. I remember once I came upon her in the garden as she stood over Bonnie's pram, shaking a rattle and cooing to her. She turned as I approached over the shaded grass and gave me a bright happy grin.

"I always wanted a sister. And now I've got one." She looked back at the baby. "Beautiful Bonnie Blue Eyes. Beautiful Bonnie Blue."

Like a fool I said:

"You mustn't grow too fond of her, Lucy."

The uncomprehending look she gave me showed just how ludicrous my words were. *Don't love too much,* I was telling her. *Don't care too deeply.* Lamely I added:

"Well, one day . . . she might have to go . . ."

"Go?" She was bewildered. "Go where?"

"Well . . ." I shrugged. "Well . . . go back . . . to her own mother."

"No, Daddy, no!" I was surprised at the vehemence in her voice. "She's *got* a mother. *Mummy* is her mother. Like *ours.* I won't let her go. Bonnie is *ours!*"

"Yes," I said after a moment. "You're right, sweetheart. Of course you're right. We won't let anyone take her away."

Inwardly I smiled at her childish aggression. But it was true—we did regard Bonnie as ours. And not as a replacement for Matthew, but very much in her own right for the individual she was. We felt she belonged. And not by dint of her comfort and the glowing reports from the social worker—but by loving and caring; she had become a part of our lives.

*   *   *

The days went by at their leisurely pace. Lucy and Davie went to the village school, I worked at my pictures in the loft and Kate stayed at home looking after Sam and Bonnie. Sometimes I worried about Kate being stuck in the house for such long periods, but she always firmly squashed any protest I made. She was all right, she insisted and, the memory of Matthew's death apart, I believe she was.

In the spring she had taken—in a small way—to writing short stories with the idea of selling them to some of the more popular women's magazines, and for an hour or two each afternoon she sat before her old typewriter and tapped away. She spoke very little about her work to me, and whenever I asked to read some of it she always hedged and put me off. "Later . . ." she would say, "later . . ." and I had to be content.

And in spite of her two-fingers-and-a-thumb method of working she met with success.

The first positive results of her labours came in the form of a cheque through the post one July morning, along with a letter of acceptance. And then, and only then, was I allowed to read the piece she'd submitted and sold. I was proud of her. It was a good story, and I must have been as excited and delighted as she was. Best of all, though, she had a new interest, and now, with the reward, the necessary encouragement to continue with it. From then on, as the weeks passed, her writing-time each weekday-afternoon became a ritual she rarely missed.

Bonnie at these times could be relied upon to sleep; she was a creature of extraordinarily regular habits, but Sam was rather a different matter. He was a mercurial boy and could sometimes be totally unreliable. So, in the end, in order to give Kate a little peace, and freedom from his time-consuming chattering and interruptions, I finally persuaded her that now was the time to have that paid assistance we had talked about.

And so we got Mrs. Gordon, a middle-aged, capable woman from the village who happily agreed to come in four afternoons a week, to keep Sam amused and out of Kate's productive way, and also to give some help around the house. The arrangement worked beautifully and Kate went on with her writing with added enthusiasm.

One thing I'm sure of, she in no way missed her acting career. Often I had felt that, by marrying her and burying her in the country, I had forced her to give it all up. But she was adamant that it no longer had any meaning for her. And she meant it.

At the start of our marriage she had kept in touch with her agent and often received letters and phone calls from directors or producers offering tempting roles in various shows. But she always, after consideration, turned them down. "Do it," I would tell her. "You want to do it, so do it." And she would ask me how I was so sure what she wanted to do, and say, anyway, that there would be time enough—and if there was not, then what did it matter?—for the present she had "enough to go on with . . ." Also, how could she leave me to fend for myself? Wasn't that what she had married me for—to save me "from a life of drudgery?" Then, of course, when Lucy had come on the scene, the possibility of Kate going back to her acting was, I suddenly saw, rather remote. At least for the time being. And so, gradually the offers stopped coming, the phone calls became fewer and eventually ceased, and her career really became a thing of the past.

On occasions our neighbour, Mrs. Hazlitt, would tell us that Kate was to be seen on television in the repeat of some play or series or film, and I would eagerly walk down the lane to sit tensed in her little sitting-room and watch Kate—a younger, different Kate—playing some pretty heroine or other. And I would be consumed with possessive pride—pride tinged with—what?—jealousy? Probably—jealous of the time before we'd met, when I had been no part of her life.

Sometimes in the beginning, with a certain amused curiosity, she would come with me, and as she watched the flickering screen so I watched her face for some sign of regret that it was all over. But I never saw it there. She seemed to view the programme much as one might go through an album of old snapshots. She made the odd comments as her memories stirred, but still she accepted it all as something long gone, beyond her present reality. In the end she hardly ever bothered to watch at all—there was always something else to do—something more important cropping up. "I've already seen it," she would tell me. "*You* go." It was plain that she was just no longer really interested.

My own work had progressed considerably since she and I had married. My talent came to be in greater demand, I was getting more interesting jobs to do and was offered more commissions than I could comfortably cope with. And really it was because of Kate; because of her and the children I worked harder; I had something to work *for*.

In a way, that year—the year after Bonnie came—really seemed ideal for each of us. All the children seemed happy, Kate got over Matthew's loss and forged ahead with her writing, and I continued, very content, with my own projects. I was in an enviable situation, I know, and I was fully aware of it. I was doing work that I loved, and when each working day was over I could go home to a wife and family who were glad to see me. I never lost that sense of excitement I experienced each day on my short homeward journey—knowing that Kate and the children would be at the end of it.

Often during the spring, summer and early autumn, I had company on my walk through the village. Lucy. So many times, when the weather was fine, I could look from my window as five o'clock approached and see her come tripping along the narrow pavement, keeping as far back from the road as possible, as she'd been taught, her face reflecting the seriousness of her purpose. She would come up the side-stairs, tap on the door, let herself in and then wait for me while I got ready to leave. Sometimes, if she was extra early, she would take paper and paints and get to work on a picture herself, soon becoming totally absorbed in her own composition and never bothering me if I had to go on with my own work.

When I think back, I don't believe she ever really viewed my occupation as *work*. Natural, I suppose. Her school-friends' fathers did things like farming, teaching, or looking after shops. Painting pictures was something you did for relaxation in school; something that was far more pleasant than arithmetic or history. I'm sure that she regarded the many pictures that I produced as the result of so much *play*.

She had a very definite artistic talent herself. Sam and Davie exhibited none at all so I was delighted to see it show in her. I would often stand above her, watching as she sprawled full-length, labouring over some particular painting. Her tongue would move over her lower lip in the effort of her concentration, and she would sing—little snatches of unidentifiable songs—the happiest sounds, her mood reflecting in her work. The pictures she made, vibrant, colourful and quite beautiful, adorned the walls all around her bed in the room she now shared with Bonnie across the landing.

Bonnie, of course, had become perfectly installed in the house, though, while the children took her presence for granted, Kate and I just couldn't. The one dark spot on Kate's horizon was the fact that, as a foster-parent, she had no actual legal claim to Bonnie. I could see how she was affected every time Miss Jenkins had been to pay one of her visits. Her periodic calls always brought home to Kate the knowledge that Bonnie was still officially *in care*—and in such a situation we had no guarantee that she would always be with us.

Our request to adopt her was really inevitable. There could be no genuine peace for us otherwise. We couldn't give Bonnie up, and we couldn't be happy in the knowledge that at any time she might be taken away.

Miss Jenkins—good, kind Miss Jenkins—gave us her whole-hearted support when we made our application, and she was with us, too, when our case came up before the judge. I didn't find it quite as nerve-racking as I'd anticipated, though I could see that Kate was jumpy and rather scared. Her voice cracked when she spoke to him and I dreaded to think what she would be like if our request was denied. I needn't have worried. Benign, understanding, he seemed quite satisfied that every effort had been made to trace Bonnie's natural mother. To our great joy he dispensed with the "parental consent" and, with a smile of congratulation, gave us his longed-for seal of approval. We had instigated the proceedings in October, and by the following May, Bonnie was ours, signed and settled. Goodbye, kind Miss Jenkins; welcome home, Bonnie Marlowe.

We had a little party that afternoon to celebrate. Kate was radiant.

It was only a couple of weeks after, on a warm, unbelievably sunny day, that Kate announced her intention of taking the children to the lake. Lucy and Davie were on holiday from school, and the opportunity, according to Kate, was one "not to be missed," and she added that *if* I had *any* sense, I'd go with them.

"How can I? I've got work to do." I was finishing my second cup of coffee before leaving for the loft.

"Leave it. It'll keep till tomorrow. You're your own boss."

I looked at her in mock surprise. "My own boss? I've got a whole gang of children to support, not to mention a very pushy wife. How can you say I'm my own boss!"

"Oh, come on." She aimed her fist at me in a slow-motion

punch, and I grabbed her hand and held it while the children clamoured around us.

"Why can't we go on a Saturday or a Sunday like everybody else?" I asked.

"That's just the *reason*. Everybody else *does* go then. And you *know*—" (Here she had the grace to grin at the transparency of her solicitousness) "—how much you hate crowds. Anyway," she added, "I don't think the weather's going to keep up."

"No, Kate, I'm sorry." I was quite adamant. "I've got far too much to do."

We left for the lake just over an hour later.

She was right—there were very few other people there that afternoon—a bit early in the season, I reckoned, apart from it being a weekday. We saw one small family we knew by sight and we smiled, nodded to them, exchanged the odd words of greeting, and then went on to make our own way round the lake. The sun was getting warmer and warmer, and I was glad I'd been persuaded to come. The half-completed painting fixed to my drawing-board in the loft seemed light-years away. Of course it would keep till tomorrow.

We made our base beneath the branches of a chestnut, some distance back from the water's edge and on the fringe of a rambling thicket that separated the lake area from fields beyond. I spread out the blanket and the picnic cloth and Kate gave her attention to the unpacking of the holdall, Davie lending a helping hand. Bonnie sat nearby, talking to herself and scratching about in the grass. Sam and Lucy had wandered off in the direction of an old oak about fifty or sixty yards away. It was a favourite tree with them. On the opposite side of the lake the other family looked very small and far away. I liked it like this—calm and secluded.

I watched Davie as he helped Kate set out plastic cups and beakers. Unaware of my gaze he went studiously about his self-appointed task, the concentration apparent in the seriousness of his grey eyes. He frowned, balancing plates and Tupperware containers. A slight breeze stirred his fair hair—so much the colour of Kate's—and I saw how the hair curled gently around his ears, brushing the collar of his checkered shirt. I thought of my own close-cropped boyhood.

"He needs a haircut, doesn't he?"

"No, not yet. It looks fine." Kate turned to Davie. "Don't you?"

He looked up from his work. "Don't I what?"

"Daddy says you need a haircut. I told him I don't agree."

"Ah," he said, and went back to his task. He wasn't interested; the problem wasn't his.

He was growing so rapidly, I realised. You were never aware of the actual growth of the children—but only of the results of it —in the shoes beginning to pinch, the wrists appearing longer from the sleeves of shirts and coats. But I saw it now in Davie. I saw, suddenly, that he was beginning to lose the roundness of his extreme childhood, his limbs were longer and slimmer. And his coordination was growing too—I could see it in his movements, his handling of the picnic things. I thought of the night before when he had sat on my knee reading to me from his school primer; his efforts to master the words, the pride in his voice when he at last solved—for him at least—some almost insurmountable problem. I thought of his own special corner in the room he shared with Sam, the space filled with objects relating to his—and only his—interests: the books, the ships and aeroplanes, the different rock samples, the pheasant's feather above the bed. He was becoming a person—separate—with his own identity.

"He's growing so," I said.

"Don't tell me." Kate shook her head and gave a wry smile. "It's frightening. I can't keep pace with his clothes." She glanced across at him and he looked up, knowing he was under discussion. "And he's going to be quite tall, I'm sure."

"I am?" Davie said.

"Yes, you," I answered.

"Well, I'm nearly seven," he said, as if that accounted for everything, and came to me, grinning, putting his arms round my neck, stifling.

I gasped for breath. "And you're getting too strong as well."

"Am I?" He turned now to Kate, stepping across the grass and enveloping her in his lean arms. "Am I too strong, Mummy?"

"*Much* too strong," she agreed, laughing as he dragged her down onto the rug. "And too big to pull me around like this."

"Yes! Yes, I am!" His words bubbled out, ringing over the water, and Kate held him against her, running a hand through his unruly hair. "Before we know it you'll be grown up, won't you?"

"Yes." For a moment he nestled there, his head on her shoulder, his mouth close to her neck. I knew the sweet smell he would smell, the soft texture of her skin that he would encounter. At my side Bonnie sat, like me, watching. She sucked her thumb, her big eyes shadowed by the leaves of the chestnut. She looked so pretty in her bright blue boiler-suit rompers. I smiled at her, putting my hand gently on her blonde curls, but she didn't look at me.

"Let's get the tea poured," Kate said, and Davie sprang away from her, reaching into the holdall and bringing out the thermos flask.

It was while Kate was pouring the tea just half a minute later that Lucy's high-pitched, terrified scream rang out.

"Oh, my God . . . !" Kate's face blanched. The cup spilled and the flask fell onto the cloth, tea spreading in a dark stain. As she jumped to her feet I was only a split-second behind her.

"Look after Bonnie!" I yelled at Davie's open-mouthed expression, and dashed away.

We found Lucy sprawled at the foot of the oak—it was obvious that she had taken a tumble from one of its branches. Picking her up I held her to me while she cried in terror at the blood that was spattering her yellow jumper. Kate, in her panic, was all flapping hands and cries of "Oh, God . . . Oh, dear God . . ." all the time. I did my best to appear calm—murmuring little safe, secure words of comfort—but what with Lucy's hysterical screams and Kate's moans, and Sam's protestations that it wasn't his fault, I wasn't surprised that I went unheard.

Kate knelt down then and I put Lucy into her arms and ran to the lake. Soaking my handkerchief in the cold water I hurried back to them. Carefully, very gently, I wiped Lucy's face so that we could see the extent of the damage. It wasn't serious.

"You're all right," Kate assured her breathlessly. "It's not much, darling." Her voice was still trembling from the panic. "You've just cut your lip. You'll be okay."

But nothing did any good and Lucy went on screaming and crying out. Shock, mostly, I reckoned—from the fall and the blood. The pain would be minor in comparison.

Only after several minutes did she eventually begin to calm down. Lying in Kate's blood-spotted arms her cries gradually died away till all that remained were little dry, breath-catching sobs. When at last she was quiet, I said:

"Next week we'll go to the circus. Would you like that . . . ?"

She nodded at me dully over her clenched hand. She was such a pathetic little sight with her face dirty and pale beneath the blood and tears, the red-sodden handkerchief held to her mouth, her eyes showing so clearly the signs of her hurt.

"Right, then," I said, "we shall go."

A few minutes later with her in my arms, her hand limp over my shoulder, we headed back for the picnic area. She seemed spent. Kate looked at her cut lip and observed quietly: "She'll need a stitch in that," and I turned and frowned a warning at her.

When we got to where the rug lay spread on the grass, the thermos still on its side with the spilt tea saturating the pattern in a shape like Australia, we looked around us in surprise.

"Now where are Bonnie and Davie?" asked Kate.

SEVEN

"They can't be far away," I said. I set Lucy down on a dry part of the rug. "I'll go and find them."

"Yes. We must get back. Better start packing up." Kate gave a frown at what was to have been our picnic, then turned and looked away along the path. When she spoke again there was a note of impatience in her voice.

"Where can they be? Davie should know better than to take Bonnie off like that."

"Don't worry. I'll find them. You go on getting the stuff together." I turned to Sam who hovered nearby impassively studying Lucy's woebegone expression. "Help Mummy pick up the cups and things. There's a good boy . . ."

Leaving them to it I went up the bank towards where the trees grew at their most dense, all the while looking about me for any sign of Davie's check shirt or Bonnie's blue rompers.

"Davie . . . Davie . . ."

There was no answer to my call and I continued on into the thicket. When I reached the heart of it—a small sunlit clearing— I shouted again.

"Davieeeeeeeeeee . . ."

Still nothing.

Beyond the slender trees ahead of me was a wire fence, and beyond that the fields stretched away into the distance, empty of all but the budding crops. I was sure he wouldn't have taken her over there. After a minute I turned back the way I had come. They would probably have returned to Kate in my absence.

Any hopes I had on that score were gone when I saw the questioning look she gave me as I approached.

"There's no sign of them," I said.

"What do you mean, there's no sign of them? They must be *somewhere*."

"Perhaps they went the other way . . ."

"Don't be silly," she said sharply. "We would have seen them."

We stood side by side looking about us, Lucy quiet at our feet. Sam was trotting away over the grass to empty the remains of the tea into the water.

"Where *are* they?" Kate no longer troubled to hide the panic that was creeping into her voice.

"I'll go and look further along. Perhaps they're hiding from us." I grasped the idea with relief. "They're hiding somewhere in the bushes, I expect . . ." I turned, moving away again.

"Well, I wish to God they'd hurry up and come out. This is no time for playing games. We've got to get Lucy to a doctor."

It was as I opened my mouth to call their names again that Sam's voice, shouting from the water's edge, stopped my own sound and sent me hurtling down towards the bank.

When I got to his side I could see her.

Bonnie lay half in, half out of the water. She was making faint little crying sounds, her hair slicked to her head, tiny mud-smeared hands reaching out for help.

In a split-second my eyes and ears took in everything—the way her elbows gouged deep into the mud, the bloody scratches on her wrists, Kate's own voice as she ran towards us; then, the next moment, heart thumping, I was leaping down over the bank. Already Bonnie was starting to slip away.

With the water nearly up to my waist I lurched forward, frantic fingers clutching, grabbing at the strap over her shoulder. I held tight, pulling her to me as I floundered in an effort to keep my balance. The mud was thick and slimy and my feet slipped and slithered as they fought to gain purchase. But I had her safe.

"Give her to me . . . !"

Drunkenly I swerved, turning full-circle, and there was Kate kneeling above me, arms outstretched, Sam and Lucy standing staring at her side. I pushed on. One foot forward . . . then the other one . . . I was against the bank, knees digging in, reaching up . . .

"Take her . . ." I thrust the soaking body into Kate's waiting arms. "She's all right. Don't worry. She'll be okay."

As Kate held Bonnie to her I tried to lever myself up out of the water. But the bank was too high and steep, and the mud kept giving way beneath my weight so that I slid back all the time. I had lost my shoes somewhere in the struggle, I realised, and now I could feel the bed of the lake oozing disgustingly under my stockinged feet. I turned and began to wade slowly along to where the bank had a more gradual slope. My progress was like a nightmare—so reluctantly the churned-up muddy water let me pass.

Up above me Kate was crying and asking how in the world Davie could have gone off and left Bonnie alone. But I was only vaguely aware of her words. I had got to the spot where the bank was lower and now I reached up and grasped at the coarse tufts of grass that grew over my head. At the same time I was groping with my feet, toes digging in, searching for a foothold, some kind of firmness.

And when I found it I cried out.

Holding on to the grass, my body shuddering, I fought to get my breath while the sound screamed out between my teeth from a throat as dry as sandpaper.

Kate's face went chalk-white. She leapt to her feet and looked down at me over Bonnie's dripping hair. And she read what was in my face—just a flicker as I hung there—but she knew. Then the echo of her own cry was cut off from me as I let go the bank and plunged down, the water closing over my ears.

I couldn't open my eyes beneath the surface. But I didn't need to. My searching hands found at once the collar of his shirt, the smoothness of his cheek.

I lifted him, and he hung in my arms like a sodden rag doll, the water that had taken him streaming from his body back into the lake. And I stood there, with the water up to my chest, shouting his name over and over, and knowing that no sound on earth would ever reach him again.

Later there was an ambulance. It was called by the family we had seen on our arrival. They had heard our cries for help.

The experts who appeared on the scene found me still work-ing—trying to pump back some life into the young, lifeless body that lay before me in the grass.

*   *   *

Somehow we got through the weeks that followed. I don't know how, but we did. Somehow we had to carry on. I still had my work to do and so did Kate. We couldn't just let it all come to a standstill. We had to manage some way.

Everybody was so kind to us. Even through our numbing grief the concern and thoughtfulness of the villagers surprised me. They seemed to do everything possible to relieve for us, by various means, the strain of our loss—no one saying very much after the initial words of condolence but showing their sympathy and affection in a score of other ways.

Like Mrs. Hazlitt, our little widow-neighbour, who called round bringing home-made bread and fresh eggs. She "just hap-pened to be passing," she lied. And then Ian Barrow and Les Hopkins, two young farmhands from the village, who also ap-peared one afternoon. Both self-conscious and bearing gifts, and both eager to get away again—to escape from the awkwardness of their shy, halting excuses for being there. Ian's wife had done too much baking, he told me, handing over a basket containing a large apple pie and a lemon-sponge cake—and "she wondered if maybe the children couldn't help her out . . ." Les brought but-ter and a box of vegetables. He knew, he said, that I wasn't "so keen on the old gardening . . ."

It didn't stop there. There was also Mr. Daniels, our milkman —due for retirement and getting slower with every season, who, for a whole month, left an extra pint of milk on our doorstep, and then swore blind that Kate was mistaken when she insisted on paying for it. Everybody makes mistakes, he told her, and went on doing it for another fortnight. And all the while, Mrs. Gordon worked harder than ever, often staying well beyond her appointed time in order to help Kate with the children or some domestic chore . . . So many acts of kindness from so many people . . .

And yet, with all their efforts, nothing anybody did could really help. Because nothing could ever bring Davie back.

Thoughts, pictures of him would come to me just a second after waking, shocking me from the forgetfulness of sleep, striking blows that were almost physical. And even in sleep I was not completely free. So often sleep brought dreams of him. And if not to me, then to Kate. There were so many times when I awoke to the trembling of her body next to mine as she cried silently into her pillow.

But during the days, of course, memory of him was *always* there. Always. So many times I watched and saw Kate simply stopped in her tracks, tongue-tied, annihilated by the ghost of him, and I'd feel the pain in my throat tighten like a cancer.

Lucy was left with a tiny hair-line scar from her tree-fall. I never saw it afterwards without seeing Davie. So much promise. All over.

For some time I was aware of feelings of resentment towards Bonnie. It was obvious to us—and to everyone—what had happened that day: she had strayed to the water's edge and had fallen in. And Davie had drowned whilst trying to save her. And he *had* saved her, I reminded myself—he had preserved her life at the cost of his own. Somehow the thought of his bravery made his death even more difficult to bear—if that were possible . . .

But how unreasonable I was, I realised. It was grief, and only that, that gave birth to my feelings. I had to thrust them from me. How could I attach blame to Bonnie—a child less than two years? As easy to blame Sam and Lucy. If they had not climbed the tree, and if Lucy had not fallen, then we would have been there to prevent such a tragedy. No, the fault, I knew, was mine. Hard to accept, but I had to try, to live with it. I had left Bonnie and Davie unattended . . .

Oh, God, there was so much conjecture. And how pointless, how worthless it all was. And no amount of examination, no amount of self-recrimination could alter the situation in any way. So the thinking, the worrying, must end. It had to stop. Davie was dead. Impossible to realise, but it was so. He was gone. From now on we must live for the living.

In time, I knew, Kate would be herself again. It was a bad patch, but we'd get through it. Be patient. Say nothing. All our memories apart, we would, given a breathing space, be as we once were.

EIGHT

"Are you sure?"

"Yes." Kate nodded. "And I'm certainly not imagining it."

Over her shoulder the warm July sun glinted on the cups and saucers of our afternoon tea. Against the light the fronds of the ferns in the tall vase looked transparent.

"But she and Sam have always got on so well together," I said.

"I know. But not lately."

We had been discussing plans for a little party to celebrate Bonnie's birthday—her third—due in a week's time, when Kate had asked whether I'd noticed a difference in Sam's behaviour.

I frowned, studying her across the table, trying to read her expression. Over the past year she had got so much better. Easier with me, and more at peace with the children. And I had been so happy seeing the change in her, seeing her more as she used to be. Now I wondered, briefly, whether the change might have been a product of my hope and imagination. But no. There was no sign of the great tension I had used to see in her face. No hint of hysteria. She just looked worried.

"Tell me what you mean," I said.

She shook her head. "It's hard to say. I think perhaps he's—jealous. Maybe he resents the attention she gets as the baby of the family. I don't know. I can't think of any other way to account for his behaviour."

"What kind of—behaviour? He doesn't seem any different to me."

"Oh, dear." She sighed. "Maybe I'm making a lot out of nothing. But he comes to me . . . keeps coming to me with stories . . ."

"What stories?"

"Stories. Tales. He keeps accusing her of things. Cruel things . . ."

"Oh, come on. Surely not."

"Darling, I'm not making it up," she said quickly. "He *does*. If it had just happened once or twice it would be okay. But it happens often."

"Such as . . . ?"

"Well . . . he says she's *cruel* to him. He says she pinches him—'hurts him' as he puts it. Lots of little things like that. And he blames her for damage to things of his that he's obviously done himself."

She moved over to the window and looked down the garden path to where Sam sat playing with his toy farm-cart. I went and stood behind her, my hands on her shoulders.

"I wouldn't bother about it. Whatever it is, I'm sure it will pass."

"It *does* bother me," she said. "It's just not like him. He's getting so—destructive. His books and things. And he blames it all on Bonnie."

Over her shoulder I watched Sam. He sat on the flagstoned path filling his cart with earth from the garden. The sun beat down on his straight chestnut hair, making it shine almost bronze where it reflected the light. Against the white of his tee shirt his arms were deeply tanned, his hands darker still with the dust of the dry earth. I had given him the cart two months ago on his sixth birthday. It had become his favourite toy and he took it with him everywhere. Looking at him, seeing him so content, so absorbed in his play, I found it hard to accept what Kate had told me.

"Well, if it's true," I said, "then it's just a phase. Forget it, Kate."

"Yes." She nodded. "I'm probably being just over-indulgent."

Late the following afternoon I found, partly concealed behind the rain water-butt, the remains of Sam's farm-cart.

Kate was busy preparing tea in the kitchen when I returned home, and I had gone back outside to take advantage of the sunshine after my day cooped-up indoors. It was as I idly pulled a few weeds from the flower-bed that I came upon the pieces of his toy. It had been wrecked beyond repair. And not by any minor accident: the wood was splintered and the metal twisted and bent.

I couldn't understand it. Sam had always been so careful, so proud of his belongings. It was a quality in him—in all of them—that we had tried to encourage. Now, looking down at what was left of his toy, I felt completely at a loss.

I went back into the kitchen where Kate was breaking eggs into a bowl.

"Where's Sam?"

"Playing upstairs, I think." She didn't look round, went on with her work.

As I got near the top of the stairs I could see over the landing to where Bonnie sat on the playroom floor. Sam was kneeling close beside her. I thought at first that they were in the middle of some game or other until, very suddenly, Sam's voice rang out.

"*No!*" he said. And I realised they weren't playing at all.

I reached the doorway just as he raised his clenched fist and struck Bonnie hard in the face.

I was so shocked I just stood there. I watched as Bonnie rocked backwards, reeling from the blow. She didn't scream or cry out. No sound at all. She just got to her feet and moved towards him while he backed away towards the window. And it was then that I yelled.

"*Sam!*"

There was a kind of shocked silence as they turned to look at me and I could hear the sharpness in my voice echo around the room. Furious, I strode forward, grabbed him, and slapped him hard on the leg.

"How could you do such a thing! She's just a baby!"

He turned to me with pain and shock in his eyes. Tears welling like sudden springs. His words choking out between his sobs.

"Daddy . . . Daddy . . . Daddy . . . Daddy, she hurt me . . . hurt me . . . Bonnie hurt me . . ."

"Rubbish!" I barked. "Don't lie to me! How could a child of that age do you any harm! She's barely three and you're six!"

"She did. She hurt me . . ." He put a hand to his head. "My hair. She hurt my hair." He could hardly speak for the tears.

"I don't want to hear any more."

We faced each other, I looking down from my six feet and he looking up at me with disbelief in his face at the expression on my own. I held out to him the pieces of the broken toy.

"How did this happen?"

He looked away, and then back again. His lips were pressed together, chin quivering.

"Answer me," I said.

His eyes flicked a glance at Bonnie and then to me. He hesitated another moment, then said quietly:

"Bonnie did it."

There was a pleading look in his eyes, as if he knew that I wouldn't believe him. For seconds he just stared at me and then, with a rush, came towards me, arms outstretched.

"Get away from me," I told him. "You're not the boy I know. You're cruel and you're a liar."

He gave me one more look: amazement, horror, then turned and ran out of the room.

I listened to his stifled sobs receding, the clatter of his feet on the stairs. Then I went over to Bonnie. She was crying now. She sat by the window making little moaning sounds, her face wet with tears. I held her to me and kissed her cheek where the imprint of Sam's hand still lingered—red and angry as the mark I had left on his leg.

"You're a brave little girl. Don't cry." I dabbed at her wet eyes with my handkerchief. One hand, I noticed, she was keeping behind her back.

"What's that you've got there . . . ?" I asked. "Can I see . . . ?"

She smiled at me at last, gave me an impish little look and shook her head. Her hand moved more firmly out of sight.

"Come on, now. Aren't you going to show me?"

She shook her head again.

"All right, baby, you keep your little secret." I patted her blonde curls. "Go on downstairs now. It's time to eat."

After she had gone I stayed for some minutes thinking over what had happened. Ah, well, it would all sort itself out, I told myself, then I went down to the kitchen and dropped the wreckage of Sam's toy into the waste-bin.

I was about to replace the lid when I saw something lying among the scraps of paper, potato-peelings and egg-shells. I reached in and lifted out a small tuft of hair. The same colour as Sam's. On the end was the slightest trace of skin, blood-stained.

I stood there. Kate entered, clattering cups and saucers. I must have looked miles away, for she said, "What are you mooning about? Have you lost something?" I didn't answer. I didn't know what to say. Then, "Come on, darling," she said, "the children are washing their hands. Tea's ready."

"Okay."

I opened my fingers and let the hair fall back into the bin and covered it with the lid. *Forget it.*

Coming from the bathroom a few minutes later I found Kate, Lucy and Bonnie sitting at the table. Kate was cutting bread. She said quickly:

"Sam is evidently not hungry, so I've sent him back upstairs. He's in a terrible mood, and I'm just not going to put up with it. He refused point-blank to sit next to Bonnie, and when I insisted he made a dreadful fuss. So he can just go without." She put slices of bread on a plate and put it in the centre of the table. "He's getting impossible, that boy."

I had been about to sit down. Now I moved back towards the door. Kate looked at me sharply.

"Now please—don't you go up and start laying on the sympathy. He's got to learn."

She was probably right. He had to learn. I nodded, went to my chair and sat down.

"Daddy . . ."

Bonnie was seated on my right, giving me a winning smile, her teeth very white against her pink cheeks. She held out to me a tiny piece of brown bread.

"For you . . ."

"Ah . . . thank you . . ." I leaned over, opened my mouth, and she put the tit-bit inside.

"What a sweetheart," Kate said. She was smiling again now.

"Yes, she is." I kissed the top of Bonnie's head. Her hair was soft and silky against my lips, and for a moment the memory of the tuft of hair I had found in the waste-bin came back to me. But it was useless to dwell on it. It didn't mean anything. Nothing at all. Bonnie's eyes were full of love as she smiled. Hold on to what is real, I told myself.

"Yes," I said, "she *is* a little sweetheart."

Lucy said, not to be outdone:

"Bonnie's *everybody's* sweetheart."

*   *   *

Later, when Kate was getting Bonnie ready for bed, and while Lucy sat reading, I went upstairs to see Sam. He was very much on my mind.

I opened the door quietly. And as I stood there I was struck again with how different it all looked since Davie had gone. Well over a year had passed, but I suppose there are some things you never get used to.

Everything that was his had long since been taken out of the room. *I* had done it. About a month after his death. Noticing one day the room's extraordinary untidiness I had suddenly realised that Kate just couldn't bear to go in there and be faced with all the reminders of him. She just couldn't cope. So I had gone in and collected up everything that belonged—*had* belonged —to him, his books, his models, his pebbles, his paints, his rock samples, his games. I filled two large boxes and I put them in the shed.

Kate never commented on the room's sudden barren appearance. Neither did I mention what I had done. When I had taken the boxes through the house she was nowhere to be seen.

A week after I saw that the pheasant's feather was still Sello taped to the wall. I took it down as carefully as if it were crystal and put it away with his other things. For all I know it's there yet . . .

And still, as I stood there, the emptiness of his corner could take my breath away. It made my love for Sam well up in me so strongly, so that, for a moment, I was tempted to wake him, to hold him. I kept thinking about the slap.

I moved softly across the carpet and looked down at him as he lay fast asleep. He had pushed aside some of his blankets—probably due to the warmth of the evening—and I pulled the sheet up more closely under his chin.

He didn't stir. I leaned down, listening to his steady breathing, peering at his face in the dim light from the window. And even as I watched, his peacefulness was punctuated by a sigh—too deep for such a small boy—that disturbed, for a second, the rhythm of his body. I reached out my hand to him. The same hand with which I had struck him.

I had never laid a finger on him before in his life. Not before that afternoon. And when I had done it then it had been in sudden anger, and without thought—so I tried to comfort myself. I was overwhelmed with remorse when I thought of it. I could still feel it—the blow. I can feel it *now*. I can still feel my hand bouncing off his flesh, the sting in my palm and fingers.

I put out my hand and lightly touched the top of his head. I stroked his hair—but very gently, so as not to waken him. And he flinched in his sleep, jerking his head away as if I had hurt him. I peered closer, straining my eyes to see.

I *had* hurt him.

Two inches from his ear was a little bare spot, bloodied, the size of a new penny. It was raw. As if the hair had been torn from his scalp.

NINE

Around the breakfast table Lucy, Kate and I gave Bonnie our birthday kisses, our greetings and our little gifts. It was a Sunday, so I could enjoy my day at home. Later on, Kate and I had planned, we would organise some games in the garden. After that, Bonnie would have her party.

Kate and I gave Bonnie a box of bricks. Lucy gave her a brightly-coloured ball which she had saved up to buy from the village shop. Sam's present was there too—a wooden boat that he had made weeks ago, now wrapped in gaily-patterned paper that was clumsily stuck together with tape. The gift lay next to her plate, but he, himself, would not go near her.

"Come on," Kate said to him as he hovered uncertainly at the far end of the table. "This nonsense has got to stop." She spoke half-coaxing, half-reprimanding, holding out her hand to him, crooking her fingers. "Come on. She's just a little girl, and it's her birthday . . ."

She paused. We all waited.

"Come on now, Sam . . ."

A week had passed since the incident with the broken toy, and during that time he had refused to go anywhere near where Bonnie was. During mealtimes Lucy had changed places with him—to Kate's displeasure—otherwise he just would not eat. But the situation couldn't continue, it was clear.

"Come on now, Sam," Kate said again, a stronger note in her voice. Lucy opened her mouth to speak, but Kate silenced her. "No, he's got to sit in his own chair. He can't be pandered to like this."

But Sam stayed where he was, eyeing the empty seat next to Bonnie. In Kate's face I could see her growing frustration.

And suddenly she moved, so quickly that Lucy started. Kate jerked from her chair and gripped his wrist.

"Now! Sit down now! Now! This instant! And stop being so silly!"

"Kate—" I began, breaking our unwritten rule that neither should undermine the other's authority, and she frowned at me so that I stopped. But she relaxed her hold on Sam's wrist.

For some moments we seemed fixed like statues, the only sounds being Kate's angry breathing and the bird-song from the garden. And then Sam was moving to the table, quiet, obedient, taking his place next to Bonnie.

We watched.

In the almost tangible silence Bonnie gave him her sweetest, warmest smile, then reached out and placed her hand on his.

He tensed. I saw his fingers clench, gripping the tablecloth, his knuckles showing white beneath their tan. Then, the next second, Bonnie leaned over and kissed him gently on the cheek.

"Isn't she sweet," Kate said. She smiled encouragingly at Sam. "Be a good boy, darling. Now kiss her back. Show her we can all be good friends. Let's stop all this silly quarrelling."

But Sam didn't seem to be aware of her words. He had raised his eyes to me, and, in the space of that split-second I saw a look of pleading there. Pleading and—what?—fear?

His glance moved back, resting on Bonnie. Without taking his eyes off her he lifted his hand and wiped roughly at the spot on his cheek where she had kissed him.

"Leave the table." Kate's voice sounded tight and level. Her eyes were blazing. "When you are ready to apologise for your behaviour you can join us again. Not before."

Leaning across the table she snatched up his plate and moved briskly away into the kitchen. A moment later she reappeared standing in the doorway.

"I've put your breakfast out on the kitchen table," she told him. "You can sit out there. See how you like eating on your own."

Sam was quite still, his eyes cast down at the empty table-space before him. Lucy looked from his face to Kate's and then back again. She didn't understand it. No more did I.

His mouth sullen, Sam paused a moment longer then got down from his seat and walked past Kate into the kitchen. Through the doorway I watched as she pointed to his plate.

"Sit down. And no more nonsense."

Forlornly he sat. The chair was rather low for him and he looked incredibly small and alone at the large scrubbed-wood table. He made no effort to eat. Tears came to his eyes and rolled down his cheeks unchecked. Kate gazed at him for a second, as if wavering, then turned and came back into the room. I saw the distress in her face, and I was angry at him for causing it. She was right. He couldn't be allowed to continue in this way.

As I ate I turned now and again to look at him where he sat, his breakfast untouched before him. I was amazed at his strength of will. But he gave in. He was probably hungry. After a while he took up his fork and began to eat, although the food must have been quite cold by now. He ate slowly, mechanically, and obviously without enjoyment, and I knew that his behaviour had been no mere gesture. Still, it was beyond me. It was almost as if, being adult, I was blind to what he, in his childish acceptance of everything, was so much aware of.

*   *   *

He ate his lunch alone, too.

Afterwards, as Kate carried empty dishes out to the kitchen she stopped by his chair, looking down at him as he toyed with the remainder of his food.

"Don't you want it?" Her tone was softer. I couldn't see her face but I could tell she was aware of the misery he was suffering.

He shook his head and kept silent. The tears were not far away again, and I knew that if he tried to speak they would fall. Kate knew it too. She put down the dishes and crouched beside him. I watched as she put her arms around him, wrapping him close. He clung to her.

"Oh, darling . . ." All the warmth was back in her voice. "You're such a silly boy. We all love you so. Don't you know that?"

He said nothing, just nodded against her shoulder, his eyes shut tight.

"I don't understand what's happening between you and Bonnie," Kate went on, "but you mustn't be unkind to her. She's only three years old. *Today*. And especially as it's her birthday. And you're a big boy. You are, aren't you?"

He nodded again.

"So, please, darling, try to be nice to her. Won't you try?"

". . . Yes . . ." He spoke so softly I could hardly hear him. He held on tighter, his fingers gripping her cotton blouse.

"Look," Kate said brightly, "we're going outside in a minute to play some birthday games. And we want you to come and join in. We want you to." She looked over at me. "Don't we?"

"Of course," I said. "It won't be any good without our Sam."

"Will you come?" Kate asked him.

"Yes." His lip quivered. He was overwhelmed by the display of much-needed affection. Whatever it was that had led to his previous behaviour, it was over-ruled by his present, stronger feelings. He'd had enough of solitude.

"Good boy," Kate said gently. "I knew we could depend on you." She kissed the top of his head, gave his shoulder a little squeeze and he looked up at her and smiled. With such relief. She smiled back and stood up. "Just let me get the washing-up done, then we'll all go out and have some fun. Okay?"

"Okay."

He got down from his chair and ran out into the yard. Kate watched him go, then turned and looked at me. She sighed, raising her eyebrows, but I could see how glad she was that he had finally come to his senses.

"I told you he'd be all right," I said.

Later, when we had stacked all the dishes away; when the dining-room and the kitchen were tidy again; when the jellies were setting and the fairy cakes were cooling, Kate and I went into the garden. Crossing the lawn I touched Kate's shoulder and pointed.

"Look at him."

On the far side of the lawn Sam swung back and forth on a

rope suspended from a branch of the stout apple-tree that supported his tree-house. Even as we watched him he stopped his swinging and scrambled up the rope, agile as a monkey, till he reached the limb above. Unaware of us, he climbed nimbly along the branch and onto the platform. As he reached it he turned and saw us. He grinned and waved.

"Come on up and play with me."

Kate laughed. "You must be joking! If you think I could climb up there you must be mad."

"It's easy," he said, with some pride.

"Yes, easy for you," she said.

"Daddy, you come up."

"Later, maybe," I answered. "Come on, we're going to the orchard. We need you to help us with the games."

As I looked up at him I recalled how I had erected the platform four summers ago. Really with Davie in mind—and how he had loved it. But only Sam would enjoy it now.

Sam was swinging from a branch above the platform, lifting his feet clear.

"Come on down," Kate said. "Bonnie and Lucy are waiting for us."

For just a moment I saw him falter in his rhythm as he swung to and fro. I tried to read his expression but his face was shadowed by the foliage. Then, making his decision, he said, "All right," dropped back onto the platform and came to the edge. Kneeling, he grasped the thick rope that hung almost to the ground and lowered himself, hand over hand, until he had reached the grass. He ran towards us and Kate ruffled his hair.

"Good, let's go," she said. He grinned, stepping out, as if he would have run on ahead, but she held onto his hand, tightly—savouring the contact, I knew.

Before we got to the orchard we could hear Bonnie's squeals of delight. We found her and Lucy chasing around among the trees and rolling in the warm, dry grass. They stopped as we approached, and Bonnie ran to us, arms outstretched, pleading to be lifted up. I chuckled and swept her into my arms, holding her there as I picked bits of grass from her new party dress. In her hair her blue silk ribbon was coming adrift and Kate said, "Hold still, darling," and retied it, more securely.

As I set Bonnie back on the grass Kate glanced up at the sky, smiling, creasing her forehead against the sun.

"It's such a gorgeous day . . ."

"Beautiful . . ."

She turned, eyes following Bonnie who now dashed off in pursuit of Lucy again. There was a gentle expression on Kate's face, the smile lingering still. Absently she lifted a hand and brushed back a lock of hair. Her eyes had a far-away, dreaming look. I wondered what she was thinking of . . . If only there was some way I could make up to her for the unhappiness she had suffered. But perhaps time would do it. I could only hope.

I sat down, the grass soft under my faded blue jeans. I patted my shirt pocket, trying to locate cigarettes, then realised I had left them indoors. I looked across at Sam: "Would you mind, Sam? . . . my cigarettes . . . ?" and he sped away, back towards the house. Kate watched him go, then knelt, picking a blade of grass and putting the end between her teeth. I moved closer, reached out and touched her hair. She smiled at me.

"What's up?"

"Nothing. Just making sure you're still there."

I took the grass-stem from her mouth and kissed her, just lightly, and she let her body rest against me. I kissed her eyes, her hair—gently—as if I would kiss away the past hurt and make everything as it was. At least, I consoled myself, everything *between us* would stay the same.

Here, in the orchard, holding her to me, I felt safe, secure. Whatever changes we had had to come to terms with; whatever changes there might be in the future, I could be sure of her love. Whatever happened, I would have Kate . . .

She had been pulling at bits of grasses and leaves—a lingering nervousness still showing in her fingers—and now she held up a little spray of greenstuff with pink flowers—"Wild thyme . . ." —and pushed the stem through a buttonhole of my shirt. "There you are . . ." She patted my chest. "Now you're all ready for the party." I looked round and saw Sam come through the gate carrying my cigarettes. Kate got to her feet and called out, beckoning, to Lucy and Bonnie.

"You're just in time," I told Sam. "You must help us decide what we shall play."

"I want to stay with you," he said.

I was about to answer, but Kate turned and gave him a warning glance.

"Sam, please. Remember what you said . . ."

Lucy and Bonnie were running towards us. When they got to us, laughing, out of breath, I asked:

"Well, what shall we play? It's got to be something nice for Bonnie Blue."

"Hide-and-seek," Lucy suggested. She pointed a finger at me, then at Kate. "But you've got to join in as well. Not just us."

Kate laughed. "Of course we'll join in."

"All right, then: Hide-and-seek." I turned to speak to Sam, and saw that he had moved away and was now swinging on the orchard gate. "How about that, Sammy?"

Bonnie, who had been holding my hand, released me and ran towards him, her face all eagerness. "Sam . . . Sam . . . Sam . . ." she chuckled, reaching up to him, her fingers touching his own.

Sam stood quite still, looking at her. Then, snatching his hand away, he jumped down from the gate and ran away up the path. Kate looked after him, frowning. Her smile was quite gone. I was annoyed. Just when everything had been going so well.

"Ah, let him go," Kate said. "I give up. If he wants to be so *stupid* . . ." She turned back to us. "All right then, who'll be first to seek . . . ?"

"I will." That was Lucy.

"Right. And no peeping." I think Kate was forcing herself to sound more cheerful for the sake of the others. Nothing must be allowed to spoil the fun. "Count to twenty, slowly," she said, "and then come to look for us." She added, as Lucy moved away:

"Can you count to twenty?"

"I should *think* so!" Lucy's voice was full of indignance. She tossed her head with a *tcchhh* of scorn, and then closed her eyes, leaning against an old plum-tree. "Starting now," she said, and began to count in slow, sonorous tones: "One . . . two . . . three . . ."

Bonnie must have played the game many times before, I thought, watching as she scuttled away, giggling, to hide, but even so, her sense of involvement surprised me in such a young child. As she hid in the long grass at the base of an apple-tree, Kate crept hurriedly away towards the bushes that ran along the bottom of the orchard. I moved back through the orchard gate and along the path to the lawn. When I got there I heard Lucy's distant cry of "Here I come! Ready or not!"

As I stood deciding on a likely place to hide, a slight movement above and to my right drew my attention to the tree-house. Sam was perched up on the platform looking down at me, his eyes peering through the screen of leaves and apples.

"Come on," I said. "Come on down. We're having a lot of fun."

He said nothing. Just looked.

"Come on down, Sam. Why not come and join us."

Slowly he shook his head.

"Oh, well . . ." I shrugged off his stubbornness. "Do as you must."

For a moment or two longer he continued to look at me, then retreated away out of sight. After a pause I moved towards the tree, resolved to climb up and talk to him, ask him Why? What was happening . . . ? I had just reached the foot of the tree when, with a triumphant shout, Lucy leapt out from among the bushes and grabbed at my shirt.

"Got you!"

She took my hand then, and led me down towards the orchard. When I looked back Sam was not to be seen.

"That wasn't really fair," Lucy was saying. "It was too easy. You weren't really hiding."

"You were too quick for me," I said.

In the orchard again it was my turn to be the seeker. Lucy pushed me towards the plum-tree.

"Now close your eyes *tight*, and *don't* look *round!*"

I said to Kate, "She's so bossy. I don't know where she gets it from. Certainly not from me."

"Oh, listen to Mr. Placid talking," Kate said. Then she added: "Have you seen anything of Sam?"

"He's up in the tree again."

"Did you talk to him?"

"Yes. He won't come down."

"I'll make him," she said, and began to move away. I stopped her.

"Leave him. Let him get on with it. Let's play our game."

Lucy was growing impatient with all the talk.

"Daddy, close your *eyes!*" She gave me a nudge in the back. "And start to count. And no *cheating.*"

I laughed, shut my eyes, leaned my head against the rough bark and began to count in a loud, slow, theatrical voice. Against my own sound I could hear the whispers, squeals and giggles as the two girls dashed excitedly away.

I counted even more slowly towards the end, trying to build up the suspense:

". . . Eighteen and a half . . . eighteen and three-quarters . . ." and at last I got to twenty, opened my eyes and yelled, "Here I come! Ready or not!"

Kate was easy to find. I discovered her crouching behind the garden shed. I said laconically:

"Really, my dear, you'll have to learn to do better than that."

"Oh, hang it all . . ." With a little laugh she got to her feet. She pulled a face. "I just don't have any imagination, that's my trouble."

"Pity."

"Yes, it is." She leaned down and brushed a smudge of earth from her knee. "To tell the truth, I'm rather relieved that you found me so quickly. That was not the most comfortable position I'd chosen for myself. Also, it'll give me a chance to look in the kitchen. I've yet to add the roses to Bonnie's cake."

"You can't go yet. It'll be your turn to seek next."

"Oh, you'll manage. And they'll understand if food is involved." She started to move away from me. I reached out and took her hand, holding her, drawing her back.

"Suppose I won't let you go . . . ?"

She smiled, shrugged. "Well, you're bigger than I am."

"Yes." She felt very slight in my arms. I caressed the soft firmness of her small breast, holding her tight to me.

"The children . . ." she muttered. I kissed her, moving my hand inside her blouse. I bent my head and kissed her flesh, sweet-scented, just above the line of her brassiere. She said again, "Alan, the children . . . darling . . ."

"They'll wait another moment," I said. Suddenly I wanted her so much. I knew I couldn't do anything about it, but I wanted her, right there. I felt her come closer to me, and I pressed my own hardness against her pliant body. "You want to as well," I said.

"Yes." She nodded, whispering. "But we can't. Not now . . ."

"No, not now." I kissed her again. "But later . . ."

Off in the distance came Lucy's voice: "You'll never find me, Daddy!"—prompting me to hurry up and seek her out, growing tired of waiting.

"There's your cue," Kate said, and I shouted out:

"Yes, I shall! Any second now . . ."

I released Kate from my arms and she tripped off through the brambles. She smiled at me over her shoulder, then disappeared round the corner of the shed. I saw that the thyme she had put in my shirt button-hole had been crushed, the scent drifting up more strongly.

Going back into the orchard I moved in the direction from where I thought I had heard Lucy's voice, peering up into the low-branched trees, looking for some tell-tale patch of colour among the foliage. Nothing. I circled the orchard again, then decided that she must have changed her hiding-place. I returned to the garden, calling out in a sing-song voice, full of melodramatic menace.

"Lucy Locket, I shall find you . . . I'm coming for you . . . Oh, Lucy . . . Oh, Looooooooooocieeeeeee . . ."

I paused every few minutes to listen for any sound of breathing or stifled giggles. But there was nothing at all. I carried on like an idiot.

"Lucy Locket, I shall find you . . ." and then: "Bonnie Blue-hoo, where are you—hooooooo? Little Bonnie, here I cu-huuuuuuuuuuuuuuummmmmmmm . . ."

At last, approaching the redcurrant bushes, I heard from their midst a little squeaking giggle, breathless with suppressed excite-ment. Leaping into the centre of the patch I pounced on Bonnie as she tried to burrow deep amongst the leaves.

"*Gotcha!* Bonnie Blue is *mine!*"

She shrieked in terror-stricken delight, her laughter gurgling, bubbling up like a spring. Grabbing her, I held her to me in a great rush of affection.

"I've caught Bonnie!" I sang out. "I've caught Bonnie!"

In my arms she giggled and chirped, her yellow curls swing-ing about her mouth. I brushed the locks back from her pink cheeks. "You've lost your ribbon," I said. I set her down on the ground again. "Come on. Now you must help me look for Lucy."

"Look for Lucy!" she echoed. "Yes! Yes! Yes!" and we moved hand in hand across the path, through the gooseberry patch, and back to the shed, but still there was no sign of her. As we approached the lawn I thought suddenly of Sam's tree-house—she might be hiding there.

It was only about seven feet from the ground, and by leaping up I could just see the rough surface of the makeshift platform. Empty.

"Where can she be . . . ?" I said.

"L-u-c-y . . ." Bonnie let go my hand and calling in her little piping voice, went to poke about in the brambles that grew along the hedgerow. "I'll find her!" she assured me. "Lucy . . . Lucy . . . Lucy . . ." I grinned at her enthusiasm and turned away.

And it was then that I saw *him.*

". . . Sam . . . ?"

He was lying near the bole of the tree, partly concealed by nettles and the long grass. He looked much too still.

"Sammy . . . ?"

The voice in my parched mouth didn't sound like my own. I felt sick.

I stepped closer, bending into the nettles, careless of the leaves that stung my hand. His soft cheek was warm beneath my fingers, but I knew the warmth was going, that it wouldn't return.

TEN

There is a pigeon hopping on the sill of the window that overlooks the patch of concrete down below. He has only one foot. Over his bobbing head I can see a corner of the Power Station and endless rows of London houses. I know I'll never get used to the view—though he seems well at home with it. He adopted us soon after we came here, arriving regularly every day for food, and we felt sorry for him. I admired his ability to survive the competition from his better-equipped mates and we fed him willingly. Not now, though. He gets no joy at all these days, and not on *that* window sill. Already his visits are becoming less frequent. He'll give up soon and try somewhere else.

That's what *we* had to do.

I had hoped—assumed—that when the inquest was over we'd be allowed to pick up the bits and pieces and try, again, to start building a new life. I knew it would be difficult—of course it would—but, in time, I thought, we could manage it. There would have to come, eventually, a time when the hurt wasn't quite so saturating; a time when Kate came back from that other world—distant, secluded—to which she had withdrawn. As it was I couldn't bear to watch her. I could almost *see* the lines of suffering in her face grow deeper. There was a great weariness about her, a lassitude, and at the same time an alarming tightness. She seemed to exist as if living on the edge of a precipice. I couldn't reach her at all.

With the children, though, it was different. She insisted on letting Mrs. Gordon go and then lavished displays of affection on Lucy and Bonnie that were almost uncontrolled in their intensity. But outside of that—her role of mother—she didn't seem to exist. It was almost as if she'd erected a shield to protect herself from further hurt.

At the inquest, held in the main hall of the village school, she was like an automaton. I had feared tears and hysteria, but there was nothing. She just sat there—even when it was over and we were free to go—staring ahead, unseeing, at the children's paintings that lined the walls.

That, of course, followed the endless questions from the police. For days on end they were in and out of the house. I dreaded their visits and I dreaded their effect on Kate. And the questions seemed to be always the same ones, always beginning with the same words: Do you remember . . . ?

Did we remember? Could we ever forget? I shall never forget the picture I have of Sam as he lay in my arms, his head lolling back, the scrap of blue clutched in his tight fist, his eyes wide open . . . Did we remember . . . ?

It is amazing how the fragments that make up those moments remain so clear with me. Everything—the sights, the sounds, the smells—as if all my senses contrived to preserve, just for my torment, the memory of it.

And when I have wondered at the change that took place in Kate I ask myself how she could *not* change. My own life felt shattered, so how could I expect Kate—particularly Kate—to be able to survive another such catastrophe? How could anything remain the same? It is a wonder—with all that followed—that she kept her sanity.

I can still see her as she ran from the house that afternoon, wearing her apron, her hair flying, coming at me like a wild woman, crazed, clutching at Sam's body as I held him, struggling for possession of him, snatching him to her. I can still see her as she sits there, rocking back and forth, supporting his head on his broken neck, her mouth opening and closing, emitting sounds like that of some mortally wounded animal, eyes staring in disbelief. I can still see Bonnie standing there, twisting her hair-ribbon in her hands and crying out. I can still smell the nettles, the flowers, the fruit, the wild thyme in my button-hole; see Lucy appearing from somewhere—her hiding place—and adding her own screams of horror. The whole afternoon was stunned, freezing itself before me for the space of moments, imprinting itself indelibly on my brain's screen.

Did we remember? What is miraculous is that a person can keep such memories and keep on living.

Kate couldn't shut herself off for long, though. Reality had to get through to her at sometime. And in the end the reality was brought home to her in ways that couldn't be ignored.

I don't just mean the press—though they certainly did their best to make our lives more miserable. I should have been prepared for them—Kate's past career made her news, of course—but I wasn't, and when they descended on us I was taken completely by surprise. They harassed us for days. One eager, bristly young man I threw out bodily after he had followed Kate from the village one afternoon, refusing to take no for an answer. My right thumb took a beating in the process, but so did his camera on the gate, so I reckoned it was worth it.

But at least they were doing a job—not like those other ghouls who made the telephone calls and sent us the letters, who were cruel simply for the pleasure it gave them.

I came down the stairs one morning to find Kate sitting on the bottom step holding the first anonymous letter in her hands. She couldn't stop shaking. When I looked at the letter I could see why.

The police know a thing or two. Don't think they don't. People are smarter than you think. Three of your children dead in three years. There is a lot of talk and not without reason. Why don't you own up? There's a lot of talk.

They varied very little. They all contained the same vile, sadistic accusations. I can see the words now, written in block capitals on cheap, lined notepaper. I wanted to go to the police about them, but Kate wouldn't let me.

From then on I made sure I went through the mail before she did—she wanted it that way, too—so she never saw the others, but she could tell when they arrived all right.

And the same with the telephone calls. She was in the room when I took the first one and she could tell by my behaviour that something was wrong. Then, when I told her not to answer the phone "for a couple of weeks," she knew. Sometimes the strange voice sounded like a man's, sometimes like a woman's, but it was hard to be sure: pains were obviously being taken to disguise it. The accusations were the same as in the letters, and, in addition, accompanied by streams of abuse—as if the other vicious attacks hadn't been enough. After three days of it I got the GPO to give us an unlisted number. We heard no more then.

The letters, too, stopped after a time. Whoever it was must have got bored with the whole thing and turned their knives in other directions, but at least *we* were free of them. I was encouraged. "You see?" I told Kate, "people are coming to their senses." I knew they would. Things would go on improving. Like everything else, it was only a matter of time.

I was too optimistic. I realised that one September morning when the four of us were sitting round the breakfast table. Kate had just asked me to go easy on the milk for my second cup of coffee and Lucy asked for more milk with her cereal. Kate shared what was left in the jug between the two girls then said, "That's all, I'm afraid, until I can get to the shop." She was drinking her own coffee black, I noticed, and where she, too, would usually have eaten cereal, she was eating toast.

"Are we economising?" I asked.

"No. Pearce didn't call this morning . . ." Pearce was the loutish young man who had taken over the milk deliveries when old Mr. Daniels had retired earlier in the year. I was silent. Kate added, without looking at me:

"He didn't call last Friday, either. He told me he forgot." She picked up the empty milk jug. "It appears his memory's getting worse." She looked at me, letting the words sink in.

"And Jarman doesn't want our apples this year."

"But he always takes our crop. He always has done. And his father did—from *my* father."

"Not any more. He sent a note round first thing this morning."

". . . Did he give a reason?"

She shrugged. "He said he's 'easing off', whatever that means . . ." The look in her eyes needed no explanation.

"This is a fine time to tell us," I said. "He was due to come and pick them over a week ago. Why couldn't he let us know sooner?"

"I suppose he forgot, too."

"But . . . we had . . . an understanding . . . always . . ."

"Then you'd better talk to him."

"Well," I said futilely, "if he doesn't want them, then he shan't have them . . ."

"Quite."

The real crunch came later. A week later.

I was painting in the loft. I had made an early start and was still hard at it some hours later. With everything that had happened—including the spraining of my thumb in the scuffle with the news reporter—I had got behind with my work. Now I was hurrying, trying to make up for lost time.

Suddenly the door flew open and Kate ran in, holding Bonnie by one hand and clutching her shopping bag in the other. I put down my paint brush, switched off the radio and went to her.

"Kate—darling, what's the matter . . . ?"

She put down her shopping and leaned against the table, tears streaming down her cheeks, her arms hanging limp. At her side the full bag of groceries tilted and smashed to the floor. She didn't move. She stood there while the milk and the ketchup poured out in a pool to saturate the bread, the biscuits and the paper bags.

"I can't—can't stay here any more," she said at last, choking on the words. "We've got to get away."

I tried to put my arms around her but she pushed me away.

"I mean it. I can't stand it any longer!"

"Tell me what's happened . . ."

"Oh, Alan, we've got to go. The people . . . the women . . . the way they look at me. The way they stare. All the whispering . . . the whispering—it's going on all the time."

She turned from me and stood facing out of the window. Her eyes were dull. She wasn't seeing the hills—only the past weeks of torture. And I knew that today's happening wasn't an isolated incident but just one in a series. And I'd known it was going on. Of course; I, too, had eyes and ears.

"All those people who were so nice to us once," she said. "They've changed. You can tell. Everywhere. Every time you go into a shop—how the conversation just—dies, and you stand there in silence and suddenly everybody's so busy you'd think that work was the only thing on their minds. And when you go past them in the street you feel them watching you, feel their eyes on your back as you go by, and you know that in another couple of seconds they'll be all heads-together again . . ."

I looked at her defeated back, and I was filled with anger at the stupidity of all those people who, so callously, were now adding to her suffering.

"Something's got to be done," I said. But I felt helpless.

"Yes." She turned and faced me. "We've got to leave. That's what's got to be done."

"Well . . . we'll see how things go . . ." It was wrong to run away, to let ourselves be driven away. How could we? The village was our home.

"We'll talk it over," I said.

"No! I don't want to talk it over! I want to go where there are crowds, where people don't look at me and whisper." She sobbed and looked down at Bonnie who sat on the floor eating a biscuit salvaged from a damp packet.

"I want to go back to London . . ."

I lived in hope as the days went by, waiting, looking desperately for some indication that the situation might change. But there was nothing. And now the maliciousness of the gossip, the rumours, and the evil from them, seemed to permeate the very house so that, even behind closed doors, we didn't feel safe. There was just no peace any more. In our bedroom Kate—as she had done for weeks past—undressed quickly and kept to her own side of the bed. When I reached out for her she bore my touch with no pleasure, her body tense, waiting.

"Kate . . ." I could tell she was awake. "Don't keep away from me."

"I'm sorry . . ." Her voice was flat; there wasn't a chance she would respond to me. "I just can't relax." She paused. "I know I won't ever be happy here again."

The anger I had felt welled up in me, full of hate. Everything I ever wanted was being destroyed. I could have run through the village streets breaking windows and shouting obscenities like a bitter, impotent child. I sat up, drowning in my helplessness, the fury and resentment coming over me like a wave, pouring into my words, and I swore and growled my hatred at the top of my lungs. *"You bastards! You bastards! Fuck you all! You bastards!"* Then reaching out to the bedside table I snatched up the porcelain madonna—*Our Love and Good Wishes for Your Happiness*—and smashed it against the wall.

*　　*　　*

And here we are. In London. Now, instead of the garden, the orchard, the village below the hill, woodland and streams and rolling green hills we have the planned acres of Battersea Park surrounded by untold square miles of bricks and mortar. And instead of the robins, the finches, the magpies and the thrushes that fed every morning on our bird-table we have a disillusioned pigeon with one leg.

I didn't sell our house. I couldn't. I just locked it up. One day, I told myself, we'd all be able to return. But I did sell the cottage with my studio on the top floor. The tenants of the flat bought it, and we made the deal quickly and they got a bargain. I couldn't wait, not with Kate in the state she was. We had to move and we had to move without delay.

We didn't waste much time searching around, either. This was only the third place we looked at. I say looked at: Kate didn't do much looking. She just came with me and wandered silently through the empty rooms, her dull eyes devoid of any interest. The desperation was there all right, though, and when I said to her yes, I thought it would do, she agreed at once. I reckoned that given the chance, she'd probably have said the same about the first place we had seen, an enormous, impossible flat in Shepherd's Bush where the adjoining pub would have spilled its drunks onto our doorstep, and where the walls throbbed with the lunch-time-noise from the juke-box that seemed to have only bass and no treble.

There was far less room here, but for the time being—until

we had an opportunity to look around for something more suitable—it would have to do.

The flat—I find it difficult to think of it as *our* flat—is actually
on two floors. On the third floor there is a small entrance hall, a
large kitchen and a very large living-room. Upstairs there are
two bedrooms, a smaller room—"Pity it's not big enough for a
studio," I had said—and a good-sized bathroom. We would manage okay. One thing, at least, there was plenty of cupboard-
space. Everything taken into account, I considered we were
pretty lucky.

When it came to finding myself a place to work, though, it
was not as easy. But after searching among the small ads in the
evening papers for a couple of weeks I eventually found a large
single attic-room in a house in Hammersmith. The light was not
as good as that afforded in the loft, it lacked the peace and quiet
I had valued so much, and I paid for it through the nose, but, I
told myself, I'd get used to it. I would have to. We all had to
make sacrifices. And I had one consolation: from the window
where I sat at my drawing-board I could look out and see the
corner of a small park, Ravenscourt Park. It was grey and bleak
when I saw it through the rain that day in November, but even
so, the sight cheered me. And the scene would improve. In the
spring the grass and the leaves would grow. There might even
be flowers.

The actual process of moving was good for Kate, I'm sure. It
was no simple job packing up our belongings after so many years
in one place—for days we were frantically busy, sorting, turning
out cupboards, packing crates and boxes—and she was kept occupied so completely that she literally had no time to think much
of other things. Also, *we were going*—and sad as it made me, for
her it was a spur. She was glad. You couldn't help but see the relief in her face. When we drove down the lane away from the
house for the last time she looked firmly ahead. There was never
a backward glance at the village, either. Only a little, almost imperceptible sigh, as if she was finally released from the weight of
some unbearable burden.

Even so, in spite of the hope that came to me, it was by no

means over yet. On our first night here she came to me as I was undressing ready for bed. I was dog-tired, and all I wanted was to lie down and sleep, and to feel the comfort of her warmth, her closeness in the alien room. She stood awkwardly just inside the bedroom doorway, a long moment in silence, wanting to speak but not quite able to.

"What is it? Aren't you coming to bed?" When I looked at her she avoided my eyes. "You must be tired."

"Bonnie's a little restless—nervous," she said at last, too quickly. "It's probably the new surroundings . . ."

I guessed what was coming. "Yes . . . ?"

"Well . . . I think perhaps I'll stay in their room. I'll sleep in her bed. I've put her in with Lucy."

". . . All right, Kate." I managed to hide the little flash of angry impatience that sparked in me and she smiled suddenly, relieved.

"Just for tonight," she said.

Just for tonight . . . I consoled myself with her parting words as I tried to settle, tried to sleep in the familiar, suddenly-much-too-big bed. Just for tonight . . .

But I slept alone again the next night, the night after that and the night after that—and as the nights went by I began to wonder whether we hadn't set a pattern that was irreversible. But no, I assured myself. No. It would pass. As I had told myself over and over in the months gone by: it would pass . . . everything passes.

Where the girls were concerned there appeared to be no problems. They had no difficulty at all in settling in. Lucy took to her new school at once and soon made friends there. Bonnie seemed happy too—but she was so young, anyway, and so eminently adaptable. All that remained was to wait for Kate . . .

And gradually she did come to terms with it all: her loss, the newness of our surroundings, her memories. The process was slow, but it happened.

It was evident first in the way she began to show an interest in the flat—painting, decorating, turning it into a home. But more important how, day by day, she loosened her obsessive grip on the girls. For weeks she had been unnaturally protective of them, continuously worrying over their safety when there was no need for it. When this began to go I knew that the rest would right itself as well. I didn't have to wait too long, either.

A week before Christmas we hung holly and paper-trimmings around the living-room and then started on the tree I had put near the window. On the rug before the fire Bonnie sat in her pyjamas, ready for bed, Lucy near her on the sofa. Together they were joining in with an old record of carols, singing *I Saw Three Ships*—Lucy's long-time favourite. The room was full of Christmas. Kate's eyes were calm. I watched her as she stretched up to put a coloured bauble on one of the highest branches, and although she frowned in the vain effort of securing it I could see that the tightness about her face was gone; there was a peace there now and I welcomed it so thankfully after its long, long absence.

"Let me do it." I moved to take the silver-pink ball from her, and our fingers brushed and she took my hand in hers, looking at me, her grey eyes steady, but uncertain, on my face.

"Are you all right . . . ?"

What a question coming from her.

A little silence fell between us. The piping voices of Lucy and Bonnie sang into it: *And what was in those ships all three—on Chri-istmas Day? On Chri-istmas Day . . . ?*

". . . Yes, I'm all right . . . of course . . ."

"Really . . . ?"

"Really . . ."

It was as if I hadn't seen her in months. We stood looking at each other. The voices of the girls, in shaky unison with the sweet-sounding chorus, filled the room . . . *All the bells in earth shall ring—on Chri-istmas Day . . .*

Apart from a single side-light, the only illumination in the room came from the fire and the tiny lights we had hung on the tree. One, glowing orange, reflected in her cheek as she looked up at me . . .

. . . *On Chri-istmas Day . . . And all the bells in earth shall ring—on Chri-istmas Day in the morning . . . !*

88

"It was the only way, wasn't it . . . ?" She meant the move from the village. "It was the only thing to do . . ."

. . . And all the angels in heaven shall sing—on Chri-istmas Day . . . On Chri-istmas Day . . .

". . . It was, wasn't it? Tell me it was . . ."

"Yes. The only thing . . ."

We stood there facing each other, almost shyly—but in those few seconds my world came right-way-up again.

When it was time for bed she went, as before, into the girls' room, but then—creeping softly so as not to waken them—reappeared carrying her dressing-gown and night-dress over her arm.

Neither of us commented on her return.

When I came from the bathroom I found her already in bed. I thought she was asleep. Till I got in beside her. And then she reached out her arms to receive me, drawing me close.

It was at that moment, as I pressed her to me, that Bonnie, in the next room, began to cry.

Kate tensed in my arms, and we waited together for the crying to stop. It didn't. After a while Kate broke away from me and sat up.

"I must go in to her. Perhaps she's having nightmares . . ."

She went out and came back fifteen minutes later with Bonnie in her arms.

"I'm sorry. I just can't get her to settle." She looked at me apologetically. "I told her she can stay with us for a while. Is that okay?"

"Okay . . ." I felt cheated.

I felt cheated even more when Bonnie crawled over Kate's body to snuggle down between us. Kate sighed. "I'm sorry, darling . . ." She looked down at Bonnie who was already drifting off to sleep. "I don't understand what's upset her."

Not long after, Kate was fast asleep too. I turned over on my side. Ah, well, there would be other nights . . .

When Bonnie cried again the following night and was brought into our room, Kate said, "It's probably a bad patch she's going through." I said nothing. She added, "We can't just let her lie there and scream. Lucy wouldn't get any sleep—not to mention us. Though don't worry—it won't go on."

But Christmas came and Christmas went, and night after night after night Bonnie came to share our bed.

It was amazing how quickly her tears dried when she was brought in. How quickly she settled down. You'd hardly have known she was there.

But she was.

So the only time Kate and I had to ourselves was in the late evening after Lucy had gone to bed and before we, ourselves, went. On two or three of these occasions when we sat alone in the living-room together I reached out for her, taking her in my arms. But that's about as far as it got. Any attempt at further intimacy just never worked. She would suddenly tighten up, tense, fearing that one of the girls might waken and come wandering out from their room; and of course it was a possibility. In the end I knew better than to try. And anyway, there was always the consolation that *this* could be the night when we wouldn't be disturbed, and as I undressed for bed I'd wait, listening, almost praying for Bonnie not to cry out. But she always did. I wanted to say to Kate, *Leave her. Let her cry. There's nothing wrong with her. She won't come to any harm.* But I didn't. I couldn't insist. After what had happened to Matthew and Davie and Sam, Kate just wouldn't take any chances.

"She's just got into the habit," I said. "She knows she can get her own way."

"Give it a while longer and she'll get over it."

"You keep saying that."

"Please, Alan—she's no real trouble . . ."

No, she wasn't. Once asleep she slept soundly. She hardly ever stirred.

Except one particular time.

That was the night when I lay awake much longer than ever. I wanted Kate so badly, and my thoughts, my needs, made it impossible for me to get to relax.

In the end I spoke her name, softly, and she answered, and I crept out of bed, went round to her side and got in with her.

We kissed. In the pale light that fell from the window I could see the eagerness in her face. I pulled her night-dress up around her waist and caressed her, pressing my near-naked body against her own, desperate for the release of long-pent-up feelings and desires.

"Kate . . . Kate . . ."

Her fingers fluttered like a bird's wings on my chest. "Oh, darling . . . darling . . ." she murmured.

And then Bonnie's voice.

"Daddy—Mummy—what are you doing . . . ?"

She was lying there looking at us, watching us.

"Nothing," I said. "Nothing . . ."

I moved away from Kate's now-rigid body, sat on the edge of the bed and pulled on my pyjama-jacket.

"Go back to sleep, baby . . ."

I tried to sound calm, reassuring, when all I could feel was resentment and frustration. What was happening? First it had been Kate, herself, and now it was Bonnie who was getting in the way.

Later, as I still lay awake, irritable and angry, Kate whispered:

"I'm sorry, darling. Really. Just try to be patient a little longer . . ."

"I'm sick of being patient," I said.

I was.

ELEVEN

"You're back early," Kate said, looking at me as I stood in the doorway wiping my wet shoes on the mat.

"Yes. That room's like an ice-house today. The gas-fire just isn't enough this weather." I took off my jacket and flopped down into my chair. "I'll get a little oil-heater tomorrow—something. It'll be okay then."

It had been snowing all day, and I'd sat for hours hunched up over my drawing-board, feeling miserable, and trying to coax a little production out of my cold fingers. In the end I'd given up. To hell with it.

"I thought they forecast milder weather for February," I said.

"They did."

Lucy brought me my slippers and I put them on—what relief. She had been cutting out robins and holly and things from a little pile of old Christmas cards, and now she went back to her task, her tongue working in the corner of her mouth as she manipulated the scissors. On the rug beside her, Bonnie was making a puzzle. I saw the concentration in her eyes as she snapped the pieces in place. On the lid of the box were the words, *For ages seven to ten.* Very bright little girl, Bonnie.

"I'll make you some tea." Kate got up and moved into the kitchen. On the dining-table I saw her typewriter, uncovered, a stack of untidy papers next to it.

"You've started again," I said when she returned, "—have you?"

She shrugged, smiled. "Well, I tried. Got to make a start some time, as they say."

"Good."

"Though I'm afraid I didn't get much done. You can't—not with a small child running around all the time . . ."

Over the tea a little later I suggested that we find someone to look after Bonnie for a couple of hours each afternoon. I almost said, *Like with Sam . . .*

Bonnie looked up at the mention of her name, her eyes going from me to Kate, then back. I grinned at her and said:

"I'm sure Bonnie wouldn't mind. And it would give you a break."

"Oh, she's all right."

"Of course she is. But you just said you can't really give your mind to anything while she's on the go." It was important, I felt, now that Kate had made a new start with her writing that she should be able to continue with it. "Maybe Mrs. Taverner would have her," I said. "Her youngest daughter is about Bonnie's age. They get on well together."

Mrs. Taverner was our neighbour across the landing, a large, good-natured, unflappable woman, mother of two young children and wife of an engineer who seemed to work nights for ever. I had sometimes wondered how his upside-down schedule affected their marriage; while he slept away the days she was always busy with their son and daughter or her clay-modelling; he rarely had a chance to be alone with her. But there, perhaps it suited him that way . . .

Kate said, after a little moment's thought, well, yes, she could certainly make use of the time, and then later—yes, perhaps it would be all right—after all, why not . . . ? and finally—okay, she'd speak to Mrs. Taverner about it.

She went to see her that same evening and returned, smiling, to say that it was all arranged. Mrs. Taverner would be very happy to help out with Bonnie ("That dear little soul? Of course!"). Also the "little something" Kate offered her for her trouble would, she had been told, "come in very handy". And there'd be no trouble with Mr. Taverner; another child in the house wouldn't disturb him. According to his wife it would take a bomb to do that.

So it was settled. For two hours each afternoon, until the time when Kate went to fetch Lucy from school, Bonnie would go over to stay and play with Mrs. Taverner's Gillian. Bonnie baulked at the separation at first, but she soon came to accept it and made no further protests. I was relieved. And the fact that Kate, herself, was willing to let Bonnie out of her sight during this time was also cause for gladness: more evidence of the grow-ing ease within her mind.

And how she made use of those two hours! She can't have wasted a single minute of them. My only slight regret was that she had no real space of her own in which to work. The dining-table just wasn't good enough; she had always to be packing her papers and typewriter away at the end of each session and then getting them out again for the next one.

And that's what gave me the idea. I would make our little box-junk-store-room into a little study. For her. A place where she could leave her typewriter and her papers and books readily available, where she could make as much muddle or tidiness as she wanted, a place that would be her own, that she could lock behind her, safe from the children.

It was just after this—the time of my idea—that she decided— with a little persuasion—to join a local Women's Guild and also a writer's circle. It meant she'd be out of the flat for two eve-nings a fortnight. It wasn't much, but I'd make the most of it and manage somehow.

I did.

First of all I sorted through everything in the room.

The crate of books and the little framed prints that were her own I let remain—they would be needed. Other things I was able—with much care so that Kate wouldn't notice them—to dis-tribute around the flat, and the few odd items which were abso-lutely no use at all and which she'd never ever miss, I got rid of. Then I set to work on the room itself.

Two evenings a fortnight, while Kate was out and the girls were asleep. Two evenings a fortnight when I worked like a madman, painting, measuring, building shelves, and always packing up ten minutes before she got back, securely locking the door behind me (no one ever went in there, anyway) and greet-ing her with all the guile I could muster. It wasn't easy, keeping my secret—not that she was in danger of discovering it herself, but because I simply wanted to tell her. But I managed.

I had determined to have it ready for the 15th March,—the

anniversary of our meeting—and I thought for a while that I'd never be ready in time. But I managed that too.

The day came. Kate made no mention of the date's significance and I went off to my studio as usual. I worked steadily until just after one o'clock and then downed tools and set off back to the flat. When I got there it was a quarter-to-two. Bonnie had been safely delivered to Mrs. Taverner and Kate was sitting before her typewriter at the dining-table. She looked up in surprise as I entered.

"What's up? Is something wrong?"

"Why should anything be wrong?"

"Well, what are you doing here?"

"Some welcome. I've got to have a reason for coming into my own home?"

"You're never back at this time . . ." She could tell from my expression that I was keeping something from her. "You always say that nothing must upset your routine."

"Did I say that?" It was all I could do not to smile.

"Frequently—of old." She grinned at me. "What is it?"

"I felt like coming home. Is there any harm in that?"

"None at all. It's a free country."

"So I was always led to believe."

I had asked that the deliverymen be here promptly at two o'clock, having explained how important it was. Now I looked at my watch. Kate looked at me.

"Well, I suppose I'll find out some time," she said.

"Some time," I answered. "Now if you'll excuse me . . ." I went from her to unlock the room. As I stood there in the doorway, checking that everything was as it should be, I heard her voice as she approached from the kitchen.

"Something's going on . . ."

Quickly I pulled the door shut and stood with my back to it.

"What have you got in there?" she asked.

"Don't ask so many questions."

I was wondering how much longer I could hold out, when I heard the ring at the door-bell. "I'll answer it," I said before she had a chance to move, and went towards the stairs. Looking at her from the top step, I said:

"Now it would please me very much if you would go back and get on with your work."

She shrugged at me over the banister, "Okay," and went. I turned and ran down the stairs.

The desk was not large, so the two men had no difficulty in manoeuvring it. But it was a long haul, and by the time they got to the top they were panting from their exertions. I murmured more apologies about not having a lift, and led the way into the room. When the desk was safely installed and the men on their way again with a good tip, I stood back for a few moments and surveyed the effects of my handiwork and planning. I couldn't help but be pleased. Then, the door once more locked behind my back, I went into the hall again and called out to Kate.

She came towards me with a pencil in her hand and one eyebrow lifted.

"Oh, I'm wanted now, am I?" Pause. "Well . . . ?" Pause. "You look like the cat that got the cream."

I said nothing. I took her hand and put the key into it and stood clear of the door. She looked at the key lying in her palm, looked up at me for a second or two, then came forward and turned the key in the lock. I watched her as she opened the door, watched her face as she stood there; and every second of my work was worth her expression.

"Well, go on in then," I said at last.

She went in, almost cautiously, while I leaned in the doorway. I saw her run the tips of her fingers over the surface of the mahogany desk, brush the newly-re-upholstered seat of the Victorian chair, open the drawers, close them, open, close . . . She smelt the flowers I had placed there, and the so-new scent of the room itself: the wood, the paint, the carpet. "Olive green," she said, looking down. She put a hand up to the shelves, shining white, that ranged the wall, laden with her own books, smiled up at the Pre-Raphaelite print—her favourite of long years—that I had dusted off and hung in a new frame. There was a calendar above the desk. She saw the date and looked back at me, remembering.

"I'm a pig," she said. "I forgot."

"It doesn't matter."

We didn't talk very much then. Not for a while. In the bedroom I undressed her and she lay naked on the bed, watching me as I took off my clothes, waiting. We were quite alone in the flat. Bonnie wouldn't be back for well over an hour.

Kate sighed against my neck, her lips soft, her hands coming round me, cool on my back. "We've got lots of time," I whispered.

"Yes . . ."

I entered into her and her fingers pressed harder, holding tight. She was as starved as I was.

"Yes," she said again. "Lots of time . . ." And drew me closer still.

*   *   *

Bonnie cried again that night.

As before, Kate brought her in to sleep between us, but after what had happened that afternoon I didn't feel so much bothered by it.

"I promise you, darling," Kate said—Bonnie was already fast asleep—"that things are going to be different."

I smiled, unbelieving. "You said that already."

"No, this time I mean it. We can't go on like this. She'll have to learn. Just give me a few more days. I promise that by next week she won't be sleeping with us together any more."

As it turned out, she was right. Though neither she nor I could possibly have imagined how it would come to be.

TWELVE

It took five days for Kate's promise to come true, and even then she didn't have much to do with it.

Returning home from the studio about half-past-five, I heard her in her new study, hammering away at her typewriter. I took off my coat and went in to her, kissed her.

"You're working late."

"Yes."

She put the cover over the machine and tidied a few papers.

"Where are the girls?" I asked.

"Lucy's in her room. Bonnie's still with Mrs. Taverner. And I'm afraid she's going to have to stay there for a while."

"Why?"

"Gillian came down with the mumps today. The doctor's confirmed it."

"Oh . . . so you think maybe Bonnie's got it too . . ."

"Well, there's a good chance. The doctor said Gillian would have been infectious for the past three or four days." She clicked her tongue. "What a damn nuisance."

"When shall we know—about Bonnie . . . ?" I wasn't very well up on mumps; I'd never had it myself and when Lucy, Davie and Sam had caught it I'd been in hospital being operated on for appendicitis. By the time I'd returned home they'd all recovered.

Kate said:

"Apparently, according to the doctor, there's a fairly lengthy incubation period. He says we won't know for another two or three weeks."

"And Bonnie's going to stay with Mrs. Taverner all that time?"

She shrugged. "Well, yes. Unless you can think of a better idea . . ."

I couldn't. And the last thing I wanted was an attack of the mumps.

Kate went past me and I followed her into the kitchen where she filled the kettle and plugged it in.

"Mrs. Taverner's *so* good," she said. "As soon as I told her the situation she insisted on keeping Bonnie there until the danger's past."

"Yes, she's very kind . . ."

"The doctor was there at the time. And he said it was a good idea if she could manage all right."

"But it's so long, darling. Two or three weeks . . ."

"Well—it can't be helped." Efficiently she set the tray for our tea—our ritual. "And it's either *she* stays over there or *you* go somewhere else. And we can't have that. Anyway," she concluded, "I can go next-door and see her any time I want to, and Mrs. Taverner can always come and get me if I'm needed. Bonnie'll be all right. Don't worry about her."

After tea, Kate went over to see Bonnie. Lucy stayed behind with me. She fed the one-legged pigeon who hopped hungrily along the window-sill, and then continued with her work on a little pink mouse she was making from scraps of felt. I helped her to attach his eyes. They didn't go on quite straight, and we laughed at his comic, wall-eyed expression. I'd have re-fixed them, but Lucy said no, she liked them that way. It was a very cosy, homely hour we spent, yet somehow it seemed strange without Bonnie's chatter and bustle. It was odd to think she wouldn't be back for at least a fortnight.

"She's getting on just fine," Kate said when she returned. "I told you she would." Apparently she'd been able to make Bonnie understand the necessity of staying put for a while. "And she knows it's not going to be *too* long."

That night was the first night for ages that we weren't disturbed by Bonnie's crying. *Well, it's an ill wind . . .* I told myself. For the first night in weeks Kate and I were alone together in our bed, able to make love, able to sleep with our bodies touching, as we'd used to. I wondered, briefly, how Bonnie was getting on next-door; whether she was crying there and, if so, how Mrs. Taverner would cope.

The next day when I saw Mrs. Taverner on the stairs I asked her whether Bonnie had cried during the night.

"Never," she said emphatically. "Not so much as a murmur, the dear little thing."

*   *   *

"So you see," said Kate, "we were right to take precautions." We sat opposite each other at the supper table. Lucy, having eaten earlier, had just gone to bed. Bonnie was still staying with the Taverners. It was exactly two weeks since she had gone into her temporary exile, and Kate had phoned me that morning with the news that Bonnie was showing the first symptoms of the illness. The doctor, calling in the afternoon, only confirmed what Kate and Mrs. Taverner already knew.

"Yes. It's a good thing you acted quickly." I yawned, sighed heavily. Kate looked at the food I had left on my plate and frowned.

"Aren't you hungry?"

"No, not really."

"You're tired, though."

"Yes." I was. And I was disturbed too, by my routine being upset. Every evening for the past fortnight Kate—and Lucy as well—had stayed over at the Taverners' until Bonnie had gone off to bed. I, in the studio, hating the thought of returning to an empty flat, took to staying on to work, sometimes not getting back till after eight or so. Today I felt dead on my feet. It had been an exhausting week. Thank God it was Friday.

"How much longer will she be away?" I asked.

"A while yet. Another eight or nine days at the very least. Ah, you should see her. Her little face all swelling up. And it looks so painful, poor dear. She keeps asking for you. But I keep telling her that you're not allowed to visit her."

I shook my head. "I only wish I could." I really missed Bonnie, and I'd be very glad when she could come back home again.

"One thing she found it hard to grasp," said Kate, "was how it's all right for *me* to go and see her, but not *you*. I tried to explain to her, and I think, in the end, she understood . . . I don't know."

"She can't possibly understand," I said. "She's much too young."

"I'm not so sure. Don't underestimate her intelligence."

"Oh, she's certainly got brains, all right." I yawned again. My eyes felt prickly from the long hours working by less-than-perfect light. My back ached.

"You've been overdoing it," Kate said. "You must be exhausted."

"Knackered is the word."

When the dishes were cleared away we listened to the radio for a while and then Kate put on some records. *La Bohème.* It was our favourite opera. But I couldn't concentrate; any sympathy I felt for poor Mimi was just swamped by my own tiredness.

"Go on to bed," Kate said. "It's Saturday tomorrow. You can sleep late." She cut Mimi off in the middle of her Farewell and put the records back in their box. "I shall join you very soon."

I looked in at Lucy as I went to bed. She was sound asleep. So would I be—in a very short time.

It can't have been much later when Kate came and crept in beside me. I surfaced for a few seconds, feeling her warmth as she snuggled up to me, heard her voice dimly, from a long way off—"Sleep well, darling . . ."—felt the touch of her lips brushing my ear. I grunted sleepily, mumbling, "Yes . . . Yes . . ." And slept.

*   *   *

I awoke briefly as she stole away from my side the next morning. When I opened my eyes she said, "Go back to sleep. I'll bring you some coffee later . . ." I spread out my arms into the warm part left by her body, thought for a second that I, too, should get up, and then drifted off again.

Later I sensed her bodily warmth against me once more. And a light kiss, kisses, on my lips, but I was only briefly, vaguely aware, comfortable, accepting all, the reality just drifting on the rim of my consciousness. Again I slept.

When I awoke fully it was to her voice as she stood in the open doorway, a laden tray in her hands.

"Oh, dear God . . . !"

At my side, so close, giving me the warmth I had taken to be Kate's, lay Bonnie. She was sleeping soundly, her arm across my chest, her mouth against my cheek.

THIRTEEN

"Don't be angry, darling," Kate said. "She wanted to be *with* you. That's why she did it."

Hours had gone by since the incident with Bonnie, and the anger was still in me, quieter now, but nevertheless there. Anger, and some other emotion—I didn't know what—simmering away just below the surface of my mind, giving me a feeling of unrest. And it wasn't due solely to the fact that I'd been exposed to a virulent—and possibly, in my case, particularly unpleasant—disease. It was something else.

Bonnie was gone again now. She had been snatched from the bed and very quickly re-lodged with Mrs. Taverner. But the damage, by this time, I thought, had very likely been done.

"I don't know how it could have happened," Kate said, "without my hearing something. But I just didn't. I'd left the front door on the latch so that Lucy could get out without disturbing me and get back in without ringing the bell and disturbing *you*—"

"The front door-catch is too stiff for me," Lucy cut in. "I can't manage it. And I wanted to go downstairs to play with my friend, Monica."

"I was in the kitchen," Kate went on. "The radio was playing. I didn't hear Bonnie come into the flat at all. I had no idea. When I asked Mrs. Taverner later, she told me she had just left their front door ajar while she slipped out to the shop. When she got back she thought Bonnie was still in Gillian's room. She didn't even know she had gone until I took her back again. She was busy—you know how it is . . ."

"Yes, I know how it is."

I was sullen and ungracious, and thought I had cause to be—though it was unfair to take it out on Kate. It wasn't her fault.

And really, I *didn't* know how it was. Perhaps, after all this time, I was only just beginning to. Perhaps . . .

Kate pressed my arm. "I'm sorry, Alan. Truly." She smiled reassuringly. "And please—there might be nothing to worry about. You'll probably be okay."

"Well, I'm sure we'll find out, soon enough."

*　　*　　*

The days crawled by, and I was looking for symptoms long before they could possibly be manifested. There was no way of knowing, the doctor told me—Marshall, the one who'd looked after Bonnie—until the symptoms appeared. Just as there was no way of counteracting the illness. All I could do was sweat it out.

And while I waited, Bonnie came back to us, no longer infectious, quite well again, and none the worse.

She was full of demonstrations of affection for me, and I took and tried to reciprocate her hugs and kisses, admonishing myself for the anger I had felt. She was a child, a three-and-a-half-year-old, little child—how could I harbour resentment towards her?—particularly when she had acted—as Kate had said—only out of love for me.

Then, a week after her return, my period of wondering came to an end.

When the swelling began—at my groin as well as by my ears—I experienced, along with the ache, almost a sense of relief. At least now I knew. Now it was just a matter of eight or nine days—according to the doctor—and then I'd feel all right again.

Eight or nine days. Not long, and they'd soon be over.

I didn't bargain for how I'd feel during those days, though. Marshall, examining me, observed that it was unfortunate, but I appeared to be "one of those unlucky few" who, contracting mumps in adulthood, took it along with "complications". If, by "complications" he meant the pain I felt, then unlucky and unfortunate were the right words.

"And what about afterwards?" I asked him.

"Well, we shall see . . ."

During that long week when I lay in such discomfort, Kate went back to sleep in the girls' room. She had to. I couldn't have borne the slightest movement of her body lying next to mine. It was agony just to turn over, and when the girls came in to see me I was fretful and anxious in case one of them might just happen to jolt the bed; I was no fun at all; I was much better left to myself.

And throughout the time I lay alone I thought about Bonnie. I never ceased to think about her. At night I was no longer bothered by her cries as in the past—I supposed that with Kate in the same room with her she no longer felt insecure—but I was very much disturbed by her *being*. Long after the time when I should have been fast asleep she was still there, an enigma, preying on my mind.

I had begun to think—really think—about all the events that had taken place since she had come into our midst, the images of the incidents standing out in my mind as bright and clear as 3D magic lantern-slides. They were not new, though, these pictures. They had been there all along, every detail, every nuance. And I had ignored them, or pushed them to the back of my subconscious. Why? Because I was afraid—fearful of the conclusion to which any examination might lead me. Our lives had, over a period, begun to sail again on an even keel, and I was loath to rock the boat. But now I couldn't help it. Now I could do nothing but let the memories and the pictures go churning over in my brain, nagging at me, refusing to let me rest.

And all my thoughts I had to keep to myself. I couldn't tell anyone. Certainly not Kate. She would have been afraid—for *me*. She would have believed that such thoughts were the wanderings of a fevered brain—pure imagination.

But it wasn't imagination. I had held Sam in my arms just after his death. I had seen his sightless eyes looking up unblinking at the sun. And I had seen the scrap of blue he held in his hand—the silk that was Bonnie's hair-ribbon.

Yet how was it possible? Such things couldn't be. I had read, from time to time, odd tales of fantasy and horror—stories of weird, fantastic happenings that never strayed from the realms of fiction. How then could I credit for an instant the possibility of some equally fantastic situation taking place in my own, very real, existence? I was an ordinary man, a commercial artist living in London with a wife and children who loved me. I knew it. What could be more desirable?—or more natural? Nothing. Except that my three sons had all tragically died within the space of three years. Coincidence? Perhaps. The word was coined just to cover such unlikely happenings. But it didn't explain them . . . Not these happenings.

Perhaps, though—I hoped, clutching at straws—my thoughts, my questions were the outcome of my illness and they would all vanish as I recovered.

No. Days passed and they were still there. I lay in bed on Sunday morning and heard the downstairs clock strike two. I sighed, shifting my position. Thank God, the pain at last was somewhat easier tonight, though my head was still throbbing. Even yet, things could look different, normal, tomorrow . . . For a while I hovered on the edge of sleep. Then my thoughts, uncertain, fraying at the edges, dissolved into the jagged pictures with their sharp colours that illuminate the dreams of the sick. And I slept.

Two days later I felt well enough to get up. The day after that I felt well enough to go to the hospital where I asked—insisted—on certain tests being carried out.

I left with my fears fully realised.

I was sterile.

That night Kate came back into our room to sleep with me. She moved against me, wanting me, I know, but I was so inhibited by my knowledge that I could do nothing. I didn't tell her the reasons for my lack of response, and I suppose she attributed it to weakness resulting from my illness. I didn't enlighten her. Perhaps later I would. Right now I didn't even want to think about it.

I got up at my usual time the next morning to take Lucy to school and then go to work. As I stood in the hallway putting on my coat, Bonnie came out to me.

"Daddy . . . ?"

I looked down at her. There was a faint pleading look in her eyes; the same touch had been in her voice.

"Yes?"

I could hear how clipped the word sounded. She said nothing and I waited for her to go on. Her lips were set tight together. She drew a breath almost in a gasp, and I saw her chin quiver.

And then I saw too that her blue, blue eyes were wet with unshed tears, ready, on the instant, to fall, and I was all at once aware of how cold I had been for so many days past; of all the thoughts and suspicions I had let come between me and my love for her. I had shut her out. Completely.

I knelt, leaning forward, so that our heads were nearly on a level. She was just a child. Scared. Sad.

"What is it, Bonnie . . . ? Baby . . . ?"

The fingers she laid on the back of my hand were slightly sticky—marmalade or jam. I looked down at her hand, dwarfed by my own, then into her open, melancholy little face.

"Daddy—" Her fingers gripped mine, tighter. Those eyes.

"What is it?" I said again. "Tell me." And then suddenly, all in a rush, she said, the tears brimming over:

"Don't you like me any more—?"

"Oh, baby . . ." I put my arms around her and drew her close to me. "Of *course* I do! I *love* you." I stroked her hair, touching the slenderness of her neck; she felt so tiny in my arms, so totally vulnerable. I thought of my behaviour towards her. I had been unbearable.

"Forgive me," I said. "I haven't been well."

"Yes," she sobbed. "Lucy said I did it. Lucy said it was me."

Her tears were wet on my cheek. I held her nearer still—for my own sake as much as for hers.

"It doesn't matter," I whispered. "It's over now."

We clung to each other for a long, long moment. She put up a hand and wiped at her eyes.

"I was a bad girl. I'm sorry, Daddy. I'm sorry . . ."

"No," I said. "No, baby, it's okay. It's all okay . . . now."

I looked round and saw that Kate was standing in the doorway, watching us. She had said nothing about my recent treatment of Bonnie but she had, I know, been only too aware of it. Now, too, she was aware that it had come to an end.

Smiling, she came over to us, and I got to my feet and she

kissed me—a little longer, a little warmer. I could see relief in her face. Hear it in her voice as she said,

"Don't be late home."

"No, I won't."

And then Lucy was there too, all buttoned up in red and white, carrying her satchel, reaching out for my hand.

"Come on, Daddy. I shan't get to school in time."

"Okay. All ready." I leaned down and kissed Bonnie's cheek. "No more tears now . . ."

"No." She shook her head, her curls bouncing.

"What's she been crying for?" asked Lucy.

"Nothing," I said. "It's nothing. Nothing at all that matters now." I took Lucy's mittened hand in mine, and together we went down, and out into the street.

Nothing at all that matters now, I said to myself as we walked along. All those thoughts I had had, all those insane suspicions— they *were* insane. I must never let them get to me again. They were just like those stories I had read: pure imagination.

A young man passed by with a girl, heavily pregnant, holding on to his arm. I thought of my visit to the hospital. *Sterile.* A little wave of panic surged in me. But so what? I thought. I had come to terms with real, greater griefs, and I could easily come to terms with *that.* And anyway, all over Britain men were going voluntarily every day asking for vasectomies. The result was just the same. Besides, it wasn't as if I were only twenty and just starting out in married life. I already had a family. I had Lucy. And I had Bonnie, too.

Bonnie . . .

I saw again her tear-stained face before me. How could I have been so cruel? But no more. It was over now. Past. Nothing. *Nothing at all that matters now . . .*

Up above, the sky and the sun were bright. The warm spell we'd been promised had arrived and was making up for lost time. At my side Lucy held my hand and waved to a schoolfriend across the road. Spring was coming. I let all my unwanted thoughts dissolve into the warming air. They had no part of all this. This was the reality.

*   *   *

May came bringing almost a heat wave.

I stood in the doorway of the girls' room watching as Bonnie scrabbled busily around, searching.

"Aren't you ready yet?"

"I'm looking for my ball. I can't find it."

"Why not bring your doll—?" I suggested.

"No, I want my ball."

"She might be glad of an outing in the park." I almost added that she'd be glad of an outing *anywhere*. I looked over to where the doll—a pretty, golden-haired miniature of Bonnie herself— still lay in her original box, untouched since Christmas. I remembered how pleased we had been, Kate and I, when we had chosen it. Then our disappointment when it had been received with a total lack of enthusiasm. Ah, well, there was no predicting children . . .

Bonnie's other toys, along with Lucy's, were all around the room, in the corners, on chests, along the shelves, all in bright groups of disorder. The walls, covered with Lucy's paintings, were equally colourful.

Bonnie gave a hoot of triumph: "I've found it!" then ran to me, following as I turned and made for Kate's study.

Kate was in the act of uncovering her typewriter, all ready to start work. Lucy, dressed for the park, stood waiting.

"Are you sure you won't come with us?" I said to Kate.

"No, really, darling. I'll take advantage of the time and get on with my story."

"It must be going well. Is it?" For days past she had gone about the flat with a lightness and gaiety that made me think of her as she'd been in the earlier years of our marriage. She was all smiles and good humour. Just that morning over breakfast she had made us all laugh by doing a very camp send-up of a full-throated soprano doing an off-key *Libiamo* that must have had Verdi turning cartwheels in his grave. Even Lucy spilling orange-juice all over the cloth hadn't been able to bring so much as a frown. She was serene.

"Tell me about it," I said.

"About what—?"

"Well, your story . . ."

"Oh, *that*." She smiled—almost a chuckle.

"Isn't it?"

"Isn't it what?"

"Isn't that what you're so—pleased about?"

She smiled again, maddeningly secretive. "Oh, my story's going all right . . ."

The girls had moved to the door. Lucy, always the impatient one, clicked her tongue.

"Daddy, we'll never get there."

"Yes, yes, we're leaving right away." Suddenly, now, I didn't want to go. But there was nothing I could do about it. "See you in a while," I said.

I was about to move away but Kate put her arms up, clasping her hands behind my neck, holding me prisoner.

"You know, you look really nice today."

"Only today."

"No, always. But especially today. Did you know that?"

"No, but I'll believe anybody who says such a thing. Who am I to call them a liar."

She made her hand into a fist. "Anybody who says different, send them to me."

Behind me Lucy gave a loud sigh. Kate released me. I said softly:

"Just you wait . . ."

As the three of us started down the stairs Kate came out onto the landing and leaned over the banister.

"Now mind you don't go filling them up with too much ice-cream . . ."

"Would I ever."

She still had that secretive look about her. I grinned up at her. "What's the matter with you lately?"

"Perhaps I'll tell you . . . when you get back."

"Tell me now."

"No. *You* wait."

On our way along the streets the picture of her smile kept coming back to me.

In the park I found a good spot beneath an elm and not too far from the swings, the roundabout and the slide. I sat down, laying my old jacket beside me, feeling with pleasure the warmth on my bare arms. Opening my book, I let it rest there, unread, on the grass. From where I sat the trees, a mass of varied greens, stretched out before me, hiding from sight the river and the banks upon banks of surrounding buildings. Lovers wandered about, slowly, partly removed from their environment by the insulation of their own caring—seeing little. Families too: the adults showing a determination to enjoy the benefits of the Sunday sunshine; their children faster, dashing about, still young enough to be surprised. There were so many colours everywhere, so many new blouses, skirts, shirts, trousers and carefully-faded jeans. The air was full of the sound of the children's voices, and that, and the warm sun, had a lulling effect on me, making me lethargic. The pigeons and sparrows searching non-stop for food knew they were quite safe around *my* feet.

Lucy and Bonnie had run off and clambered onto the roundabout. I called out: "Hold tight," and: "Be careful now . . ." hearing myself sounding like an over-protective mother hen, and they stopped their chattering for a moment to call back: "All right, Daddy . . . Okay," their words changing a moment later into excited gasping giggles as they sat, gripping the metal hand-supports, going round and round and round. I wanted to shout: "Not so fast—" but managed not to. Stop fussing, I told myself. They were perfectly fine.

I picked up my book after a while, putting on sun-glasses to stop the reflected glare from the pages. The glare was about the only thing I was getting from it—a thriller that was failing to thrill. But I plodded on, looking up every now and again to check on the girls' whereabouts and safety.

When they tired of the roundabout they turned their attention to the slide, and I went over and helped Bonnie up the steps and then waited ready to catch her as she slid down. "Again! Again! Again!" she kept saying, laughing, gasping with excitement. She kept me quite busy for ten minutes and I was glad when at last the ice-cream man came round.

After the ice-creams they picked flowers—dandelions, daisies and buttercups, and I went back to my book, moving further into the shade. It was impossible to concentrate, though, and in the end I gave up and just sat idly watching as Lucy made a daisy chain to go around Bonnie's neck. Bonnie was attempting one as well, and though her efforts were less spectacular than Lucy's, still, for such a small child she showed remarkable adroitness. They talked away as they worked, an endless stream of childish chit-chat. I lay back with my jacket under my head and closed my eyes.

I was aware of their voices for some while as they busied themselves over the flower-jewellery—their words a gentle, whispering drone, soporific, blending with the other voices all around. Somewhere, off in the distance, a cuckoo called. But then, as the warmth and my own lethargy got to me, so the sounds faded and I dozed off.

I must have slept for well over an hour. When I opened my eyes again most of the family groups round about had gone or were going; dispersing in little clutches of threes, fours and fives, wandering tiredly towards the exits and tea-time. Voices called irritably to young stragglers. Dogs bounded ahead, still full of life, and were called to heel and attached to leads. I looked at my watch. Getting on for six. High time we were going home as well.

Bonnie and Lucy were over by the swings now. They were the only ones there, and neither paid any attention to me as I sat up in the shadow of the tree. I rubbed my dry eyes, shook the creases out of my jacket and picked up my book. Then I looked back again to call out that it was time to leave.

And the sight that met my eyes brought me springing to my feet, my voice ringing out hoarse and loud in horror.

"*Lucy!*"

I was only just in time.

At the sound of her name she turned to me, her head moving slightly in my direction. A matter of inches, but it was enough.

The heavy seat of the swing, hurled with what seemed to be unbelievable force and precision, just skimmed past her.

Had I not attracted her attention, the hard, wooden edge would have caught her full in the throat.

FOURTEEN

As it was, Lucy wasn't aware that she had been in the slightest danger. She stood up, smiling, and came towards me.

"What's the matter, Daddy?"

The swing had swung back now, no longer a threat, and I shrugged, feigning casualness. "Nothing. It's nothing . . ." My heart was thudding like a steam-hammer. "It's time to go home," I said.

She looked up at me with curiosity in her face. She chuckled. "You've gone all white-faced."

"Have I?" I forced a laugh. "Perhaps it's because I need my tea."

She nodded, then knelt and finished buckling her sandal. I saw the way her straight brown hair fell untidily about her cheeks; I saw the sheen on it from the late afternoon sun, watched her as she stood up, looked round and called to Bonnie.

"Come on, Bonnie. Tea-time . . ."

Bonnie was standing perfectly still. Between us the swing moved back and forth, but slower now, losing momentum, as harmless as the pendulum of a clock. Across the short space of grass and asphalt she looked into my eyes. I tried to read her expression, but there was no telling what was going on behind that wide, steady gaze.

But there was one thing I was sure of: all those thoughts I had had, all those dreams that had plagued me, all the notions I had dismissed as the crazy ramblings of a sick, grieved mind—they had all been born of reality. I hadn't been imagining things. I hadn't been mad. Everything I had considered and rejected—it was *all real*. Now I *knew*.

And Bonnie knew that I knew.

Lucy called to her again.

"Come on, Bonnie . . ."

We watched Bonnie standing there, her daisy-chain about her neck. The swing came to a stop, and for some moments the whole afternoon seemed still—as if holding its breath. Lucy called again, then turned to me.

"What's the matter with Bonnie, Daddy? She won't come."

"She'll come," I said. I put out my arms and drew Lucy to me, sweeping her up against my chest, holding her tight. Over her shoulder I looked at Bonnie. Bonnie looked at me. Still with my eyes upon her I turned my head slightly and kissed Lucy's cheek.

"Are you my girl?"

"Of course." She pressed her cheek to mine.

A hardness, a coldness crept into Bonnie's eyes, and I was aware suddenly that Lucy was struggling against me.

"Daddy, I can't *breathe!* You're holding me too *tight!*"

"Sorry . . ."

I set her down on the grass, released her. To Bonnie I called softly:

"Come on, Bonnie. Time to go home."

For a second longer she studied me, and then, bringing a warm smile to her lips, ran towards us, arms wide, all childish, bubbling eagerness. "Time to go home," she echoed.

On the way along the street Lucy walked at my side while I carried Bonnie in my arms. I would have let her walk, but I was anxious to get back. I must talk to Kate. I had to. Somehow I would have to tell her. She would think I was crazy, I knew, but somehow I would have to make her see the truth. I dreaded the confrontation, but I had no choice. *She* had to know as well.

Against my shoulder Bonnie rode, chattering and giggling in my loveless arms. I didn't listen to her. I was thinking of Kate— of her happiness when we had left her earlier on. And I was thinking of Lucy.

Whatever else happened, one thing was sure: Bonnie would have to go.

*   *   *

"You're mad," Kate said quietly. And she looked at me as if I really were. There was no trace now of all the humour, the lightness, that had been in her face. She just stared at me across the table as if I were some insane stranger, some *thing* completely foreign and absolutely distasteful to her. I reached out to her where she stood arrested in the act of smoothing the cloth, but she moved quicker than I, snatching her hand out of the path of my own.

We were alone in the room. Earlier I had crept into the girls' room and looked at them as they lay asleep. Above Lucy's pillow was a picture of *Mummy on Her Birthday*, and next to it a picture of me *At Work Drawing*. Lucy lay still, breathing gently, knowing nothing of the turmoil going on within me. In the next bed lay Bonnie, her eyes shut tight, no frown or furrow marring the smoothness of her round, angelic face. I turned away from her and, summoning up my courage, went to Kate and told her what I believed. What I knew to be the truth.

"I saw it happen," I said. "I *know*."

"Saw it happen!" she said derisively. "You saw *nothing* happen. You're making it all up. Don't think I haven't noticed the way you've been going on these past weeks! You've been so—resentful, bitter!"

"About what?"

"It's obvious, I should have thought. Because of the business with the mumps."

"No, Kate, no. That's only *one* thing. And something that you regard as an accident but which *I* believe was coldly calculated. She *wanted* me to catch mumps. And she made sure I did." For a moment I was tempted to tell her what was the result of my illness, but I decided not to—she really *would* believe I was speaking from resentment and bitterness then. "I'm not talking about that," I said. "I'm talking about what happened this afternoon."

"Stop it. Stop it *now*."

"You've got to listen," I said. "You can't just close your eyes to it. I was *there!* I *saw* it! Lucy was kneeling by the swings, buckling her sandal. I just happened to look up at *that moment*. I saw Bonnie take the seat of the swing in her hands and pull it back as far as she could. I saw her *take aim*. And then she let it fly. But with force, I mean. Such *force*. I yelled out to Lucy just in time. It was incredible!"

"Incredible. Exactly."

"You must believe me, Kate. I'm *not* making it all up."

"And where—" she asked, "—when all this was going on, were all the other children and parents?"

"There *was* no one else close by then. People were leaving. And even the few still around weren't interested in watching a couple of kids playing on the swings. Don't worry—Bonnie chose her moment."

Kate shook her head. "It's the most ridiculous, cruel accusation I've ever heard."

"No," I said. "If Lucy had been hit—and very likely killed—it would have been put down to just another accident. The result of a childish prank by a small girl who didn't know any better; a small child who did silly, unthinking things like any normal child. But it's not like that. Bonnie *does* know better. She knew what she was doing. And she's *not a normal child.*"

I watched for any flicker of credulity in Kate's face. But there was nothing. I said, hopelessly, for the tenth time:

"I saw it happen."

"Well, you're wrong! You're wrong about her. I know her. She's just like any other child—except that she's more advanced —much brighter than average. She'd never have done such a thing on purpose. Even if it *did* happen—which I doubt—she didn't mean Lucy any harm. I know it. She *loves* her."

"Yes," I said bitterly, "—the way she loved Matthew and Davie and Sam."

There was a silence.

"I can't believe you mean that," Kate said softly. "You're not serious. You can't be."

"Yes. I am."

I let it all come pouring out—all the thoughts that had stayed in my mind, never settling, never fading with the days, never allowing me any peace for long—everything that had been stored there, just waiting to be unloaded and exposed to the light of day. And as I talked even more of the pieces fell into place. Everything became clearer and clearer, even to myself, all of it making the most horrifying sense.

One accident was understandable, I said. But three fatal accidents stretched coincidence beyond the limits. And that afternoon, before my eyes, there had almost been a fourth. Could she explain that? How could any of it be explained? It couldn't just be brushed aside with our twentieth-century logic and need for scientific reasoning. Our sons had been killed. And Bonnie had murdered them.

I went back over it all.

What about the marks we had found on Bonnie's wrists when Davie had drowned in the lake—? Those scratches—"Davie made them," I said. "But *not* when he was trying to rescue *Bonnie*—when he was trying to save *himself!* For God's sake, can't you see?" I heard my voice rising while the feel of his limp, sodden body came back to me so palpably that I almost choked on the memory. "She pulled him in and *drowned* him!"

"*No!*"

Kate put her hands up to her ears and I went to her, took her arms and held them down to her sides. I had to go on, and she had to listen.

"Sam—" I said. "What about Sam? He would never have fallen from his little tree-house. Christ, he could climb those trees like a monkey! And to fall—and break his neck—just like *that* . . . ! I swear it couldn't have happened. He spent hour upon hour climbing that tree, and it wasn't even as if his tree-house was very high off the ground. No! Bonnie did it! She killed him!"

I must have appeared as deranged as Kate thought me: my face was wet with tears, my voice rising high in fury and despair at all that had passed.

"Bonnie did it! While we were all playing hide-and-seek she climbed up onto that platform. She killed Sam and pushed his body over the edge."

"She was too small!" Kate cried. "She couldn't have climbed up like that. She was physically just too small!"

"Then she did it when he was on the ground, and made it

look as if he had fallen. She—she broke his neck—and left him lying there beneath the tree . . ." I gazed at the incredulous horror in her eyes and added:

"I found Bonnie's hair-ribbon clutched in his hand. Later—I don't know when—she must have taken it back again."

Kate wrenched herself from my grasp, but she couldn't stop me talking and I kept pressing on.

"Just before he died we thought he was behaving strangely towards Bonnie. He *was*. He was afraid of her. No, not afraid— *terrified*."

I told her then of the incident when he had complained of Bonnie pulling his hair, when I had found them together in the nursery, and how, later, I had discovered a piece of his hair in the waste-bin—a piece torn from his scalp. "She had the strength," I said. "She had the strength for it all. Sam told the truth when he said she had wrecked his toy cart. She did do it. It needed unnatural power for such a small child, but she's got it. She proved that this afternoon. But I wouldn't believe Sam. I thought he was lying. But she did it. She did *everything!*"

"For God's sake, stop!" Kate shouted. She turned and swept into the kitchen. I followed. She reached the sink and whirled to face me again.

"You keep talking about Sam and Davie and Matthew, and I don't *want* to talk about them! They're gone! Gone . . !" She turned back towards the clutter of cutlery and dirty dishes. "All I've got left are Lucy—and Bonnie. And now you're trying to turn me against *her*."

"The reason there's only Bonnie and Lucy left," I said, "is because Bonnie murdered our other children. It happened, Kate. You won't wake up and find it's all been a nightmare. It's real. Your daughter almost died today."

"I don't believe you."

There was no getting through to her at all. Determinedly she turned and made herself busy at the sink, running the hot water, rinsing dishes, squeezing in the washing-up liquid. I stood watching her, seeing the sag of her shoulders that belied her dismissing words. With her back to me she said:

"You're making Bonnie out to be some kind of awful—*monster*. How can you. You've only got to look at her."

"Yes. She's the picture of innocence. As innocent-looking as a new-born chick." A thought came to me suddenly. "Do you know what the cuckoo does—?"

She moved to face me. "—The cuckoo—?"

"Yes . . ."

"What are you talking about? Now you're on about *birds!* I think you must be ill."

"I heard a cuckoo this afternoon. There was something about its call that—that—stirred something in me. I know now what it was . . ."

"Yes, you're ill," she repeated. "You're ill."

"Listen," I insisted. "Just listen to me! There's something different about the cuckoo. It's not like other birds—"

"My *God!*" She moved her hands so quickly, in such a wild gesture, that soap suds flew in small white flecks like snow. "I don't believe this conversation! I just don't believe it!"

"The cuckoo doesn't build a nest. You know that, don't you—?"

"—So—?" Her voice had taken on a note of false tolerance, as if she were humouring somebody slightly off-balance.

"No," I said, "instead—she—the female cuckoo—finds another nest, waits till it's unguarded, then lays her egg in it and flies away."

"If you're trying to give me a nature lesson," she said disparagingly, "you're a bit late. I learned all this in junior school."

I nodded. "So you know. You know that the owner of the nest hatches the cuckoo's egg along with her own. And that when it's born, the baby cuckoo does everything possible to make sure it gets the best of everything. And that means *everything*—food, space, love. It needs it all in order to survive. So what happens to the other eggs?—any other chicks that hatch out?"

"You're the teacher." Her voice was full of disdain.

"I'll tell you. Any eggs that are unhatched the cuckoo chick just heaves over the side of the nest. And if any of the other chicks have already hatched then it does the same to them too. *Out!*"

"Good boy," she said witheringly. "Now go to the top of the class."

"Whatever happens," I said, "not one of the eggs or the other chicks gets a chance. They all die. The cuckoo chick is born with one deadly instinct—to kill off any possible rival. And it does just that. Kills all of them. It only rests when, at last, it's got the nest to itself. That, and the complete and undivided attention of its foster-parents. Only then is it happy—content."

Silence. We stood there looking at each other. And gradually the disdainful expression left her face, to be replaced by sadness and strain. When she spoke she sounded pathetic, lost and frightened. I had exposed her to another kind of reality. One she could not possibly live with.

"Alan . . . please . . . Please stop. I don't know what you're saying . . . and I don't want to know." She began to cry, twisting the handle of the dish-mop in her nervous fingers. "It's all a nightmare. You said it isn't, but it is."

"It's real, Kate."

"It *can't* be! Not in *life!* That's in books. It doesn't happen to *people*. Not real people. We live in London . . . London. We're ordinary people. How could such a thing happen to ordinary people!"

"I can't explain it . . . I don't know how."

"But—but—Bonnie—Not Bonnie. Not Bonnie. *Please.*"

She threw herself into my arms, her wet, soapy hands holding on to me tightly. I soothed her—tried to—wrapping her close, stroking her dishevelled hair.

"Don't cry," I whispered. "Don't cry, darling. It'll be all right . . ."

"How *can* it be all right?" She was weeping against my shoulder. "How can it when you've just said all these things—? It *can't* be—*ever*."

"It will be," I said. I paused. "Later."

She looked up at me. "What do you mean?"

"Well—Bonnie must go away."

She stared at me incredulously.

"NO!!!"

Shrieking out, she tore herself from me, backing up against the sink. "She's our daughter. *Our daughter!*"

"She's *not our* daughter!" I shouted. "God knows whose daughter she is, but she's *not ours!*"

"She *is!*"

"No, Kate. She never was. She never will be."

"But I've looked after her. I've loved her as much as if she were my own. I fed her from my own breast. She's a part of me. She is! And you can't send her away! I won't let you!"

"Bonnie's got to go," I said through gritted teeth. My voice was unsteady, but I was full of determination. "And *soon.*"

"*Never!*"

For a second she was facing me, then the next she was rushing past me, out through the kitchen doorway and into the hall. I turned and watched as she swept Bonnie up into her arms.

How long had Bonnie been standing there at the bottom of the stairs? How long had she been listening? I saw her cling to Kate, heard her wail as it rang through the flat.

"Have I got to go away, Mummy? Have I? Oh, don't let Daddy send me away! Don't! Oh, Mummy, please don't!"

"Hush, darling," Kate said. "No one's going to send you away. Not our Bonnie. Not my Bonnie." She looked at me over Bonnie's golden curls, repeating her last words with a look of hatred and disgust.

"No one."

FIFTEEN

Lying sleepless that night on my side of the bed, I listened to Kate's breathing. She was awake too. Our bodies didn't touch.

I thought about all that had happened that day. I thought of her secretive happiness before I had left with the children for the park; and her words—"Perhaps I'll tell you . . . when you get back . . ." I thought of her warmth then and her coldness now. And I marvelled again that things could have reached such a pass.

Perhaps I'm really asleep, I thought. Like she had said—it was all a nightmare. Soon I would wake and find that all the horror had been just a bad dream—some dreadful dream that would vanish with the sun-light and the voices of my four children, Matthew, Davie, Sam and Lucy . . .

No. I knew it was all too real. Matthew and Davie and Sam were gone forever.

Beside me in the bed Kate's breathing was all too controlled. There was no rest in our London flat. We had come here seeking comfort, forgetfulness and peace, and here we were, like strangers in a railway-carriage. No rest. None at all. Certainly not for me, knowing that in the next room my daughter slept next to a golden-haired, rosy-cheeked assassin.

Yes—I said to myself, lying there in the darkness—Bonnie must go. But how? Kate would never *let* her go.

So I made my decision. If Bonnie did not go, then *I* must take *Lucy* away. And at the first opportunity. To hell with the consequences, all I knew was that she had to be taken to safety.

Kate hardly spoke to me all the next day, keeping her words down to the bare minimum that would suffice to get across any necessary information. On a couple of occasions I tried to bring her round, but it was no good, and in the end I stopped trying.

When bed-time came I became aware that she was showing no signs of going up to our room. She didn't want to sleep with me, I realised. I watched her for a few moments as she sat in the chair opposite my own, seemingly engrossed in a novel.

"Aren't you tired?"

She didn't answer.

"Kate . . . ?"

She said quickly, still looking down at her book:

"I just don't feel like going to bed."

". . . Why . . . ?"

A shrug.

"Tell me why, Kate."

Her lips were set, eyes steady on the page before her. She wasn't going to answer. After a while, I said:

"Perhaps it would be better if . . . if I made up a bed for myself down here . . ."

She looked at me then. But coldly.

"You must do as you wish."

"It isn't what *I* wish," I said quickly. "I just can't get near you. I can't reach you. Any attempt to hold a conversation with you is like pushing treacle uphill."

"I should think you'd said enough after yesterday. I'm surprised you've got anything left to say."

"Kate, why don't we stop all this? Please. We've never been like this together in our lives before."

She answered sharply: "You never threatened to take one of our children away before!"

I sat helplessly wondering what I could do, what I could say to make her see that there was reason in the incredible story I had offered her. Her voice cut into my thoughts.

"You know where the spare bedding is."

". . . Yes . . ."

From a cupboard I took sheets and blankets. I got my own pillow and then arranged it all on the sofa. She looked up from her book, watching me in silence, but made no offer to help. There was such a barrier between us now that I could think of nothing that would dissolve it.

Later, when I looked around, I found myself alone in the room. She had gone upstairs—just gone—without even a word.

I lay back on the makeshift bed, fully dressed, feeling lost, unhappy and totally bewildered. Above me I could hear the sounds of her slippered feet as she moved around the bedroom. And suddenly I realised that I must act tonight. Her need for solitude had given me the perfect opportunity.

In the dark I made my plan, then after a while I put on the light and sat up, smoking, waiting for the time to pass.

At last I got to my feet. It had been silent up above me now for quite some time. The clock told me ten to one. Very quietly I moved about the room collecting things into a hold-all. I did it slowly, careful not to make the slightest sound. Nothing must waken her.

In the hall I put down the bag and slipped on my raincoat, making sure the car keys were in my pocket. Then, conscious of the very sound of my own breathing, I crept silently up the stairs and eased open the door of the girls' room. Noiselessly I moved across the carpet and switched on the light above Lucy's bed. She slept soundly, not stirring as the warm light lit the soft lines of her face. I bent closer to her and breathed her name.

"Lucy . . ."

She didn't move. I spoke her name again, closer still at her ear, at the same time touching her shoulder. I waited breathlessly as she stirred, her eyelids fluttering, then watched impatiently as she settled back into sleep again. I shook her gently, whispering imperatively in the stillness.

"Lucy, wake up . . ."

Sleepily her eyes opened and she looked up at me, uncomprehending. Her gaze widened. I put a finger to my lips.

"Ssshhhh . . ."

I looked round towards Bonnie's bed and assured myself that she was asleep. I said, very softly, but clearly:

"Lucy darling, I want you to get up. But quietly. So, *so* quietly . . ."

"Is it morning yet?" She frowned slightly.

"No, not yet. I'll explain later. Be a good girl and don't ask any questions now . . ." I saw the perplexed expression still on her face and added, forcing a smile, "It's a secret."

She smiled at me, drowsily, then closed her eyes and turned, ready to drift off once more. Quickly I lifted her into a sitting position. "Don't go back to sleep, darling. You've got to get up."

"Why?" Her own voice came in a whisper.

"We're going out." Putting my hands under her arms I pulled her from the warmth of the sheets and sat down beside her, supporting her on the edge of the bed. She sagged against me, her arms reaching up to curl around my neck.

"Come on. Hurry, please. There's a good girl . . ."

I dragged two blankets from the bed and wrapped them about her. Standing up, I lifted her into my arms. She was warm and soft against me and just for a second I held her close, aware of her vulnerability, how precious she was to me. Her breathing and the weight of her body now told me that she was asleep again. Quietly, so as not to disturb her, I turned and reached out to the lamp. It was then I saw that Bonnie was wide-awake.

She lay there, her eyes looking into mine above the pink line of the sheet. There was a little smile on her face—barely discernible, but *there*. She knew what was happening.

For an instant panic surged in me—she would cry out—she would yell for Kate—! But then, just as swiftly, the fear dissolved. No, she wouldn't shout. She was *glad*. I was taking Lucy away. It was just what she wanted.

I tore my eyes from her steady gaze and switched off the light. When I left the room just seconds later I didn't even bother to close the door behind me. Bonnie wouldn't raise the alarm.

At the foot of the stairs I fumbled in the dark with the chain and the big key of the front door. Lucy was still asleep—so heavy on my left arm, but I didn't want to put her down. There'd be time enough for her awakening.

Damn the catch! It wouldn't budge under my fingers. I cursed myself for not having fixed it weeks ago as I'd continually told myself I must. I switched on the hall light—had to risk it—and put my shoulder against the wood in an effort to release the lock. Still no good, though Lucy, jolted suddenly awake, opened her eyes and stared about her in surprise.

"Where are we going, Daddy? What's happening?"

"Ssshhh. It's a secret, I *told you*." I tried to hint, with my whisper, of secret treats in store. Make a game of it, I thought.

"Yes," she nodded, "a secret," and yawned. "Let me get down. Can I?"

"Okay . . ." There was no reason now why not, and the door needed both hands.

"Is Bonnie coming with us?" she asked as I set her bare feet on the mat.

"No."

"Where's Mummy?"

"Sssshhh!" I said sharply. "Don't waken her. She's asleep."

Following my words the door-catch snapped back with the sharpness of a pistol-shot. I looked round in alarm and Lucy, seeing the fear in my face, cried out in panic.

"I don't want to go. I want Mummy!"

Next moment she was off up the stairs.

I took the steps three at a time and grabbed her just as she reached the landing, my hands catching her roughly about the waist. She gave a cry of surprise and fear, but I didn't hesitate as I swept her up into my arms. Just as I turned to make my way back down again I saw a hairline of light appear down one side of Kate's door. It didn't matter now that Lucy wailed, "I don't want to go! I don't want to!"—Kate was awake and all I could do was to get down to the car before she caught us.

At the foot of the stairs the front door yawned. I snatched up the hold-all and, with Lucy struggling frantically against me, hurried over the threshold. I turned immediately then and tried to slam the door shut behind me—give Kate something to cope with, delay her pursuit—but I couldn't manage it and, angry at the wasted moments, I dashed on towards the stairs. Half-way down the first flight I knew I would have to move even more quickly: behind me, very clearly, I could hear Kate's cry of alarm. Lucy heard it too, and screamed out in answer.

"Mummy!"

Her head bobbed on my shoulder with each jolting step I took. I held her roughly, desperately, while the panic that enveloped me communicated itself, meeting her own panic, so that she cried out even louder. As I started down the second flight, Kate's screams echoed in the well of the stairs. She wasn't far behind. I moved faster still.

"Mummy! Mummy! *Mummy!*"

Lucy was sobbing and shrieking hysterically now, and her voice joined with Kate's. The stairway rang with their screams. I dashed on down, forced to stop at the first-floor landing in order to get her in a more secure position. And it wasn't easy. She struggled and squirmed in my grasp and it was all I could do to get her back in my arms again. "Be *quiet!*" I said through gritted teeth. "I'm not going to hurt you." But she kept on, shouting, screaming and crying, while up above, and coming closer all the time, came Kate's running footsteps, her voice shrieking out, "Stop! Alan . . . stop . . !"

I couldn't. I mustn't. One flight to go. Turning, I headed down the stairs towards the main hall. I still had a chance. I was only yards away from the front door—and then, suddenly, my way was barred—by the old man who lived in the flat on the right.

He looked very small, and very nervous. He had appeared all at once, standing in my path, his gnarled hands with their whitened knuckles holding his dressing-gown tight around him. But he was brave all right. I must have looked like a lunatic.

"Get out of my way," I barked at him.

"What's going on here?"

His voice trembled slightly, like the hand that reached out and grabbed my sleeve. I shook him off.

"Go on! Get out of the way—"

I tried to push past him, but he moved to block me again. Over to the side I could see his wife standing framed in a dimly-lit doorway, her hands up to her face. Behind me came the sound of Kate's slippers as she flew down the last flight of stairs. The next second she had reached me and Lucy was torn from my arms. She clung to Kate, crying with fear, while over her head Kate looked at me, with hatred. I stood foolishly clutching the hold-all, panting from exertion and emotion, and mentally cursing my clumsiness and stupidity. I wouldn't get another chance. Kate would see to that.

A couple of minutes later I climbed back up the stairs and, following in Kate's footsteps, walked behind her over the welcome mat.

Back in the flat she installed Lucy in the same bed as Bonnie. I saw Bonnie's eyes flash resentment, though she put her arms around Lucy and snuggled up to her. Lucy lay crying still, her breath coming in little short, sobbing gasps. Kate watched the scene for a moment, then turned to glare at me as I stood in the open doorway. Going past me into our bedroom she returned carrying her night-dress. On the landing she stopped, facing me.

"It's all yours." She nodded back in the direction of the room that had been ours. "I shall be sleeping in with the girls from now on."

"Kate—" I said—though I had nothing to say. I let my voice tail off.

"You realise this is the end for us." She spoke bitterly. "I don't know how you think you can ever put this right."

I didn't know either. I continued to look away from the hatred in her eyes, and she stepped by me and moved into the dimmer light of the girls' room. As the door closed behind her the snap of the catch rang in the silence. I knew that nothing I said could change anything now. Not now. Not in the slightest way.

After a time I put off the lights and went into our bedroom. I lay down on the bed. But I didn't sleep. I couldn't. Something had to be done. And soon.

*　　　*　　　*

The next morning Kate said abruptly as we finished breakfast:

"I'll be taking Lucy to school."

"Kate, listen—" I began. She cut me short.

"I don't want to listen to anything you've got to say. You

don't make sense any more. You're a different person. I don't know you any more."

I sat silent, the toast before me growing cold and turning to leather on my plate. I pushed it away. Glancing up I saw that Lucy was looking at me. She hadn't spoken to me—not a word—during breakfast. I watched now as she dropped her eyes and moved closer to Kate. How could I ever hope that she might understand . . .

A few minutes later Kate, Lucy and Bonnie had gone from the flat. In the quiet I sat still and poured myself more coffee. It was cold, but I drank it anyway.

Before I set off to the studio I oiled the lock on the front door. A day too late, of course, but still, it was one of those jobs that had to be done.

SIXTEEN

On Wednesday when Kate and Bonnie returned from taking Lucy to school they found me still in the flat. I was speaking on the phone. I had waited, listening for the sound of the front door—the signal for me to begin my act—and then launched into the middle of a perfectly one-sided conversation. Kate gave no outward indication of listening to me as she began to collect up the breakfast dishes, but I knew she heard every word I said. She was meant to.

"Yes," I said into the mouthpiece, "of course I can get down to see you. It's no trouble at all for me . . ." I paused, hearing just the dial-tone in my ear. ". . . Well, as soon as possible, don't you think? . . . Yes, tomorrow would be fine." Another pause—convincing, I hoped. "It'll take me a couple of hours to get there. I could be with you early afternoon . . . All right, for lunch, then . . ."

When, my palm sweating, I had replaced the receiver, I turned to Kate as, carrying a loaded tray, she started off in the direction of the kitchen.

"I'm going down to Cheltenham tomorrow. Marianne Shaw wants to talk to me about a couple of new books I'm to illustrate." I didn't often consult with the various authors whose stories I worked on, but it did sometimes happen. I had chosen this particular writer now as she was confined to a wheel-chair and our only possible way of meeting would be for me to go and see her. "I'll probably be back about five or six . . . She's anxious to—"

"Why tell me?" Kate said, abruptly cutting me off. "You know your own work and what you have to do. I'm not really that interested."

Her reaction, at the moment, was all I could have wished for. She accepted my story without the least hesitation. Too readily: it was only too clear that she *wasn't* interested. She carried on into the kitchen and I followed and watched her as she worked, tight-lipped, unloading the tray.

"Kate, I'm sorry," I said.

I wanted to make her believe that I wouldn't try another happening like last night's. And also I still hoped, in some way, to get her to listen to me so that I could cancel the plan I had in mind. But there was not the slightest softness in her determined expression and I could see I would be wasting my breath.

"I'll see you later," I said. She didn't answer.

When I went to get my jacket I found Bonnie sitting on the hall floor working on a building-blocks-construction that any eight-year-old would have been proud of. She looked up at me and grinned, sitting back on her heels.

"Goodbye, Daddy."

She spoke purely for Kate's benefit, I knew, keeping up her act of the innocent, misunderstood child. I had a sudden, insane urge to kick out and send her brick-towers falling, but I restrained the impulse and hurried out.

I called at the bank on my way to the studio and drew out a considerable quantity of cash. Then went on to sit before my drawing-board and try to work. It was almost impossible to concentrate, though, and when I surveyed my output at the end of the day it seemed to me dull and lifeless and far less than my best. I returned to the flat to spend long, dispirited hours where the conversation, when it wasn't stilted, was completely nonexistent, and where the only uninhibited sound came from the radio. The evening seemed interminable, rigid with tension, and several times I felt the sweat—triggered by my own thoughts—break out under my arms. I had little appetite to eat the dinner that Kate silently served, and she made no comment as I shuffled the food around on my plate. When it came time for bed she went, as before, into the girls' room.

I did not even have the satisfaction of knowing that one day she would understand everything; that she would realise I had acted in the only possible way. I could only prove to her that I was right by allowing Lucy to remain there and die. And that I couldn't risk for a single day longer.

In the morning I stopped Lucy on the landing as she came pink and fresh from the bathroom.

"Lucy . . ."

She said nothing, but looked at me warily.

"I didn't mean to frighten you the other night," I said. "I wouldn't ever hurt you. You know that."

After a moment's hesitation she nodded.

"No," I went on, "never. I'd never hurt you. You don't really think I would, do you?"

She shook her head. "No."

"Good. I love you. Will you forgive me for scaring you like that?"

"Yes, Daddy . . ."

I stooped and held my arms out to her. She came to me and I held her close. I kissed the top of her head. The hair at her temples was still damp from her wash and she smelled faintly of soap and toothpaste. She held on to me for seconds after I took my own hands away, and I knew then we were all right again. As she went away from me into her bedroom I felt as if a great weight had been lifted from my mind. How she might feel towards me in the future I didn't—wouldn't—consider.

A while later I looked down from the window and watched as the three of them set off up the road. Kate wouldn't dream of leaving Bonnie alone with me now while she took Lucy to school. But that was okay with me. If I never had to set eyes on Bonnie again I'd be glad.

Turning from the view of their retreating backs, I got to work. Swiftly. I packed two suitcases with Lucy's and my own clothes and, hurrying downstairs, stowed them away in the boot of the car. I had to be quick as the school was only a short distance away and Kate and Bonnie would soon return. But I managed everything in time, and when they did get back I was tying my tie before the glass. I was not wearing my usual working-gear of denim jacket and jeans, but a tweed sports-coat and dark cords: an outfit suitable in which to visit one such as Marianne Shaw—I had to play the role fully.

As I looked at Kate's reflection beyond my shoulder our eyes met and held for an instant. It seemed to me that she opened her mouth to speak. But whatever she had been going to say she thought better of it, and the moment passed. She turned away and went upstairs. I picked up my brief-case, my raincoat, the car keys, and I was ready.

I found her in the girls' bedroom, making the beds. I stood in the doorway and watched her as she moved briskly about. Perhaps there was still time—still a chance to let the light of this incredible reality stop the corrosion that was destroying us. No. When I said, "—I won't be too late back . . ." she just nodded and went on smoothing pillows.

I drove first to my studio and packed into the boot of the car all the working materials I thought I might be likely to need over the next few weeks—assuming I could ever get my hands to stop shaking long enough to use them. I hoped, prayed, that what I had in mind wouldn't take that long, but I had to be prepared for all contingencies. Locking the studio securely behind me, I set off back in the direction of Lucy's school.

* * *

"She's in Miss Blandings' class."

I walked along the warmly-polished corridor with the headmistress, Mrs. Aldrich, at my side. She was a straight reed of a woman with a kind smile and a taste for heavy jewellery. The carefully-casual waves framing her face bounced slightly in rhythm with her energetic, springing step. A couple of minutes earlier, facing me across her office desk, she had seen at once from my expression that something was wrong, and accepted immediately the story I gave that there was a "little personal family difficulty . . ." Then, with my murmurs of "illness" and "close relatives", she had reacted with a kindness and sympathy that left me feeling a heel for lying to her. But it had to be.

Now she stepped in front of me, tapped on a glass-panelled door, opened it and went in. I followed.

The gentle hum of children's voices hushed as we appeared, and eager faces looked up with bright expectancy. Lucy sat close to the window, I saw, and she looked across at me and gave me a very small, shy smile. At the same time the girl who sat behind reached forward and gave her a little nudge in the back. Miss Blandings—not more than twenty-three and all straight dark hair and loose woollies—came towards us.

"Lucy's father has come for her," Mrs. Aldrich told her, and then beckoned to Lucy to come forward. "Pack up your work, dear, and bring your own things with you." Lucy, colouring-up, but enjoying (I could tell) being the centre of attraction, stood at her desk, collected her books together and put them away. "And your coat, dear, don't forget," Mrs. Aldrich went on. "Your daddy's come to take you home."

While Lucy went self-consciously to the rows of coats hanging at the back of the room, the headmistress turned to Miss Blandings. "Lucy won't be back for a day or two," she flicked at me a little sad smile of understanding, then added: "I'll explain later."

Outside in the corridor I held Lucy's satchel while she did up the buttons on her mac. "That's it, my dear," Mrs. Aldrich nodded, "it's none too warm out today." She accompanied us then to the main doors. As we shook hands she said, "I hope everything turns out all right . . ."

I answered, "Thank you. I hope so too." I did, desperately.

"What's the matter?" Lucy asked me as we crossed the playground hand-in-hand. She seemed to have got over her fear of the other night and now appeared quite excited at the idea of being taken out of school in the middle of class. She looked up at me with large, soft, enquiring eyes. "What's up, Daddy? Why have I got to go home?"

"We're not actually going home," I told her. "We're going away."

"Away?" The thought made her chuckle. She gave a little skip. "A holiday? It's too early for a holiday. It's not half-term till next Monday."

"And you're all on holiday then?"

"Yes, for a whole week."

Well, that was something. At least I wouldn't have to worry about her schooling for a few days.

"Where are we going?" she asked.

I wished I knew. "You'll see. You just wait till we get there. You'll like it."

There was a sudden palpable hesitation, a faltering in her step at my side, and I saw the wariness back in her face.

"Don't worry," I said, smiling to dispel her fears, "we're going to have a lovely time." Then the tightness vanished and she relaxed again. "Come on!" I said, generating her excitement, "we've got to hurry!"

We passed through the school gates. I unlocked the car and Lucy got into the front passenger seat and I buckled her in. She was all smiles and twitters.

"Nobody at school goes away for holidays this early in the year," she said. "Are we going for a long time?"

"A little while." I switched on the ignition, put the engine into first and pulled away from the kerb. When we turned right onto the main road, she said quickly:

"What about Mummy and Bonnie? Aren't we going to collect them? We can't go without them."

"No . . . we'll be seeing them later."

"When?"

"In a day or two."

"Tomorrow?"

"Well—three or four days."

"When we're there?"

"Yes."

"Why?"

"Well—first Mummy's got to finish off some work. Some of her writing. Then she and Bonnie will join us."

This appeared to satisfy her—at least for the moment, anyway. I turned to look briefly at her, aware that I mustn't allow her to see any signs of fear or tension in my face. I could see none reflected in her own. She seemed happy and excited still. I grinned at her.

"You wait, later we're going to stop and buy you some nice new clothes. Wouldn't you like that?"

"Really?" Her eyes sparkled. She was so completely feminine —always, from a much younger age showing a real concern over her appearance, always insisting on "looking nice". Now, the sudden prospect of new clothes was very appealing.

"I'd like a new dress," she said.

"You shall have one. New shoes, too, perhaps. Who knows?— maybe even *two* dresses." Why not? I asked myself—I had a wallet full of money and credit cards.

We stopped at a large department store—happily for me it was fairly crowded—and selected a number of purchases. Lucy had new shoes and her two new dresses, as well as a selection of underwear, socks, a blouse and skirt, and slippers. It would be enough to go on with; we could buy whatever else might be required when—and if—the need arose. Carrying the packages between us we headed back to the car and drove away.

She talked happily for some while as she sat beside me. She was obviously delighted with our purchases. For her, I could see, there *was* a holiday atmosphere about the trip. Later, her chatter stopped and I realised she had fallen asleep. I took my hand from the steering wheel and gently smoothed the top of her head. Her hair was very soft under my palm. Nothing must happen to her, I told myself grimly. Nothing *would* happen to her. I wouldn't let it. And to that end I was determined that she and Bonnie must never be allowed to live together again. Because all the time they were alone Lucy would be in danger. And who could watch over her every single moment? No, whatever happened I had to protect her and this, for the time being, was the only way I could think of. I didn't see that I had any choice, not right now. In a while, perhaps, we'd be able to go home again. Kate would surely see, by my present actions, that my words couldn't be taken lightly. She would have to take me seriously. She would have to listen to me now. She would have to *try* to believe me. And she would have to give Bonnie up. Just as *I* had been given no choice, so I would give Kate no choice.

But even so, I wondered, supposing she refused? Then we

might never return. And what if Lucy never saw Kate again? I pushed the thought away, it was too disturbing, but it came back, persisting. What would happen? Certainly Lucy would resent me for it—probably hate me—once she had come to realise what I had done—that I had taken her away from her mother. She wouldn't understand my reasons, of course. I sighed, gripping the steering wheel. So be it. If it was the only way. It was better that Lucy learned to live without Kate than not to live at all.

Following the traffic signs, I set my course for the motorway. Birmingham was a big enough city.

* * *

I found us a room in a small, brightly painted bed-and-breakfast house in Edgbaston; the house the only bright spot in a grey-looking street which, if it had seen better days, surely hadn't seen them within living memory. It wasn't what I would have chosen, but the first two places I tried were full, and I was too tense and nervous to keep looking.

The room Lucy and I were shown into was, so I was assured by Mrs. Hooper, the landlady, the best room in the house. It was also, she added, the largest. I'm sure she spoke the truth, but what she didn't take into account was the amount of furniture she'd managed to cram in there. After allowing room for the chests of drawers, the wardrobes, the two beds, the numerous unmatching chairs and the tables of varying sizes—and all set against a background of the busiest floral wallpaper I'd ever seen —there wasn't that much space for actually moving about. The walls themselves were dressed with at least twenty pictures of the worst Victorian vogue, while the surfaces of the inelegant furniture were laden with what seemed an unending array of empty biscuit tins, obviously chosen for their decorative lids depicting ladies in crinolines and fluffy kittens with ribbons around their necks. Mrs. Hooper was Welsh, and although she ventured the information that she had lived in the house "for donkeys' years", she still managed to sound as if she were on a day-trip from the

Rhondda Valley. She had wispy grey hair, a sharp nose, and a ferocious little mouth which, when smiling, somehow managed to completely transform her otherwise rather forbidding exterior.

I gave her enough cash to cover three days, though I said we probably wouldn't be staying that long—I fervently hoped so, anyway. We were, I told her, going on to meet my wife—for a holiday.

When she had gone Lucy said:

"Whereabouts are we going for our holiday, Daddy?"

"You wait and see . . ."

"Is it a surprise?"

". . . Yes . . . meant to be . . . Anyway," I said after a moment, "I'm not absolutely certain *myself* where we're going. It depends."

"On what?"

". . . On Mummy." And God knew that was true enough.

She nodded, turned and began to study the pictures on the walls. They seemed mostly to be of angels in varying poses of prayer or flight. I wasn't at all sure how I'd cope with them, though Lucy appeared to find them fairly amusing. I took another look around the room, and knew I'd never ever be able to work there; I wouldn't even bother taking my art materials out of the boot of the car. But apart from that I'd manage to put up with it for a few days—as long as it was only a few days. At least the beds seemed comfortable to my touch and everything around looked clean. Lucy's contentment—as far as it was possible—was the important thing, though.

"You okay, sweetheart?" I asked her.

"Yes . . ." She was intent on a picture of two angels—one with an obvious squint—who hovered gazing down over a rather ill-proportioned Christ Child. She looked at it with her head on one side for a moment longer then moved towards the window and surveyed the scene outside.

"The street is so ugly."

"Yes, it is. But, as I told you, we won't be here long."

"Good."

"Even so, this is a big city. A famous city. There are all kinds

of things for us to see." I couldn't think of anything at that particular moment, but there had to be.

"How soon do you think Mummy will meet us?" She smiled
suddenly. "I knew we couldn't be staying *here*. There isn't room
for all of us. Not with Bonnie as well."

"Yes," I said. She repeated her question.

"When will Mummy be able to meet us?"

"I can't say yet . . ." I could see there'd be many such questions. "Do you feel tired?" I asked her. "We could go out later—
and find a nice restaurant."

Her face brightened. "A restaurant! Yes!" Eating out was
something of a rare treat for her. "Can I wear one of my new
dresses and my new shoes?"

*　　*　　*

That night I looked at her as she lay sleeping in the bed fur-
thest from the door. The book she had bought in the town lay
on the bed-cover where she had left it. I picked it up and put it
on the bedside table.

So far everything had been slightly less traumatic than I had
feared. But it was only the first day, and as yet I had accomplished nothing apart from getting her away. I had a great deal
to do yet.

I got into my pyjamas and climbed into bed. I had a paper-
back beside me, but I knew it would be useless to attempt to
read it—I'd never be able to concentrate on two words together. I
reached out and turned off the lamp with its hideous pink
shade, shut my eyes and tried to will relaxation to come over me.
But I could only think about what I had done—and about Kate
and Lucy—and Matthew, Davie and Sam. And Bonnie. I fought
against my thoughts for what seemed hours, and then eventually
gave in to them. At last I slept.

*　　*　　*

Mrs. Hooper woke us at nine with our breakfast, which she
brought in and placed on a table near the window. It was boiled

eggs, toast and marmalade and tea—and surprisingly good. After we had eaten I went to the bathroom along the landing and ran a bath for Lucy. While she was soaking I stood at the wash-basin and shaved. I didn't know what I was getting ready for, but it was a ritual that killed a few more minutes of the time. I wondered what Kate was doing—how she was doing. She would be almost out of her mind with worry, I knew, and she'd never rest until Lucy was back with her again, safe and sound. Well, that had to be on my terms.

That afternoon Lucy and I went to the art gallery. Studying the Pre-Raphaelites there I thought of the print I had reframed for Kate's little study. How long ago and far away it all seemed. Had that really been us?

When we got outside I found a telephone kiosk with a tele-phone that worked, asked Lucy to wait outside for me, took a deep breath and dialled Kate's number.

SEVENTEEN

"Bring her back, Alan,—please."

I hadn't bargained for how I'd feel, and I was surprised to find my legs were weak and my palms were wet with perspiration when I heard the anguish in her voice; it came so clearly over the line. I didn't answer for a second and she said quickly:

"Are you still there?"

"Yes, I'm here."

"Please. Bring her back home. You must."

"I can't."

"What do you mean, you can't?"

"Not while Bonnie's there. Lucy just wouldn't be safe, and I'm not taking any more chances. I told you what I think—what I *know*—but you wouldn't believe me."

"How *can* I believe you? How could *anyone* believe such a thing?"

"It's the truth, no matter how—how fantastic it might sound. It's the truth."

"No, Alan, it's not. You can't *say* that. It's *insane*."

"You think *I'm* insane."

"Of course I don't. But I do think you should . . ." Her words tailed off. I prompted her:

"What? You think I should what—?"

"I think you should get some help. You need some help. Talk to somebody . . ."

"I'm talking to *you!*" I said bitterly. "As I've *tried* to talk to you. You wouldn't listen."

"Not me. Somebody who *knows*. A doctor or somebody . . ."

"I'm going to hang up if that's all you can say." I meant it.

"No! Don't! Please! Have you no idea of what you're putting me through? Don't you care?"

"I know," I said. "Of course I know. But it's a matter of Lucy's *life*."

"Alan, I just don't know anything any more. I only know I

want Lucy back. I want her back. You've got to bring her back!" Her voice became shrill. "You've *got to!*" She began to cry. For a few moments there was only the muffled sound of her sobbing.

"Yes, I'll bring her back," I said, "—when you agree that Bonnie must go."

"How can— We've been through this before—"

"I'm not interested—" I could hear my voice rising and I forced myself to sound more controlled. "I'm not interested in whether we've been through it all before. I'm telling you now that I'm not bringing Lucy back until Bonnie goes. *Then* I'll bring her back to you. Only then."

"My God!" she shrieked at me, "how can you be so cruel! Never mind *me*—think what this is doing to *Lucy!*"

"She's okay," I said. "I'm looking after her. I'm protecting her. And it's the only way I know how to. You don't think I'm en*joy*ing this!"

"Alan, *please*—!" She was sobbing openly now. "Tell me where you are. Where are you? Tell me!"

"I can't. But Lucy's all right. She's quite happy and, what's more, she's safe. And she will be as long as she's with me."

"She's *my* child, too!"

"Yes, Kate—and so were Davie and Matthew and Sam." At the memory of my sons I felt anger and bitterness well up in me so that I gripped the phone, shouting through gritted teeth, tears of rage springing to my eyes. "Get rid of her! That—that *monster!* We've got to get rid of her!"

"Alan—Alan—there are *ways* . . ."—she was almost incoherent—"There are ways to *make* you bring her back."

I'd been waiting for this. "No," I said, "—not if you mean going to the police. You wouldn't get much help there; they don't like to get dragged in. Why should they be involved?—I'm not breaking any law."

There was a little silence. She said:

"I—I just want Lucy home again."

"Yes, and I've told you the conditions. So think over what I've said. I'm telling you. I'll call you later on."

"Alan! Wait! You can't—"

I watched my hand replace the receiver on its rest, and I stood there, shaking. I'd never get her to understand.

When I looked round at last I saw Lucy's face close to the glass. I summoned up a smile and went out to her.

"Who were you talking to?" she asked.

"What—? Oh . . . it was just . . . business . . ."

She grinned, took my hand. "I thought you were phoning Mummy. Don't forget, when you do, that I want to talk to her."

"No, I won't forget," I said.

"I wonder what she's doing now . . ."

"I wonder . . ." Kate was suffering, that's what she was doing. She was going through hell. But I couldn't think of any way it could be avoided. And whatever the outcome she was going to be unhappy.

*   *   *

Later, after we had eaten, and when Lucy was settled with a jigsaw-puzzle, I slipped out of the house to the corner phone-box to call Kate again. She answered so quickly and with such anxiety in her voice that I knew she had been waiting for my call. She started at once by begging me to bring Lucy home.

"I've told you my terms." I spoke as calmly as I could. "You've got to choose."

"Choose?"

"Yes, choose. Bonnie or Lucy. Which is it to be?"

"How can you ask me to make a choice!"

"I have," I said. "And it was very easy."

"Why have I got to choose?" she burst out. "I don't *want* to choose. I want them both. Their place is *here*, with me—us—in their *home*. They belong here. Both of them!"

Christ!—would she never understand! "Not *both* of them!" I cried out. "If I bring Lucy back to you she'll—she'll be *dead within a year!* Just like the *others!* The same thing will happen to *her!*"

"They were accidents! How can you blame such things on a small, innocent child!"

I sighed. It was all such old ground now. We were like gramophone records repeating the same predictable phrases. I said wearily, "Choose, Kate. I've told you. You've got to choose which one you love most. Bonnie or Lucy. I shouldn't have thought it would be so difficult for you."

She was crying again now. "Of course," she sobbed, "if it came down to it then it would have to be Lucy. That's natural. But I love Bonnie. I love her. And she knows only me. I'm the only mother she's ever known. How could I do such a thing to her—? What would happen to her?" Her words were punctuated by the sounds of her crying and I pressed the phone closer to my ear in an effort to make out what she was saying. "Why are you doing this to me?" she asked. "Do you hate me so much?"

"Kate, Kate—I love you. You know that. I love you. I want to make you happy. It's what I've always wanted. But I can't do it at the expense of Lucy's life."

Her sobbing grew quieter. I said evenly:

"I want you to call the authorities and—and tell them that we want them to take Bonnie away. Tell them we can't look after her any more." I paused. "Do you hear?"

"She's not a foster child any longer. She's *our* child. She's legally our daughter as much as Lucy is. She's got *your* name. She's our responsibility."

"There's got to be some way," I retorted grimly, "and I'll find it. Even if I've got to dump her on somebody's doorstep. After all, that's what her mother did to us."

"Don't! Don't talk like that!"

"I mean it."

"You couldn't do anything so—heartless."

"Listen," I snapped back, "I've learned a good bit about heartlessness these past few years. You've got to realise that I mean what I say. She's got to go. You've got to agree to it. I'm not bringing Lucy back until you do. Until Bonnie's *gone*."

"How could I do that to her? How could I even *tell* her . . . ? She's so dependent on—" She broke off, very suddenly, and I knew, beyond question, that Bonnie had appeared there in the room with her. "What's up?" I asked. "Is she there?"

". . . Yes. She just came in." There was a muffled murmur—probably as she spoke to Bonnie—then her voice came clear and breathless into the phone again.

"I—I can't talk . . . Not now . . ."

"No, it's time for you to *do* something."

"Oh, Alan . . . Alan . . ." She began to cry again, desperately. I hated myself for my hardness, but I couldn't give in. I daren't.

"I must see you," she said at last. "I must. We've got to talk about this—properly."

"Talk isn't getting us very far."

"Oh, yes! Yes. You've got to give me time. I need time to even get used to the idea. I must see you! *Please!*"

"You've got to be prepared to listen then," I said. "And I'm telling you now that you'll still have to make a choice in the end."

"I'll . . . I'll listen . . ." she said. "Tell me where you are."

"I'll come and see you."

"But—"

"That's all I'll agree to."

"All right . . . When . . . ?"

"Tomorrow."

"What time?"

"About lunchtime."

". . . Right. And don't—don't . . . *do* anything in the meantime . . ." She was afraid that I might take Lucy out of the country, I thought.

"Don't worry," I said. "I won't do anything in the meantime."

It seemed ludicrous to say goodbye. I just said, "I'll see you tomorrow then—between twelve and one," and put down the phone.

When I got back to the house I knocked on Mrs. Hooper's door and asked her if—with the understanding that I paid her for her trouble—she would look after Lucy the next day while I went out. She beamed and said she'd be glad to. Strange how that smile transformed her.

*　　*　　*

Apart from a small sigh and a touching little fleeting sadness that clouded Lucy's face for an instant, she showed complete acceptance of the necessity of my "business trip" the next morning. "I'll be back as soon as I can," I told her and drove away, leaving her waving to me from the window, Mrs. Hooper standing at her side.

I got to the flats before half-past eleven and sat in the car, watching the front door and the windows, smoking and thinking.

What would we say to each other when we were together? I wondered. Did she think she could talk me round? Was she relying on my compassion? my integrity? my good sense? Could I get her to see the truth—and to agree to what had to be . . . ? Somehow I doubted it. And I knew that it might come to my having to take Lucy right away—for good. I dreaded to think what such an action would do to Kate; how she would suffer. So much more than she was suffering now—and she'd already suffered enough for twenty people. She would hate me for ever. But she would surely do that anyway. Yes, that was one thing I was sure of: it was the end for Kate and me.

Still, perhaps I was thinking too far ahead. I must at least give her the chance. I flicked the end of my cigarette into the road and got out of the car.

I didn't go straight in when I got upstairs. I rang the front door-bell and waited. I could hear no sound at all coming from the other side of the door and I rang again. At last, the tension building up inside me all over again, I took my key and let myself in.

I called out—tentatively—but there was only silence. The rug at the foot of the stairs had been pushed untidily to one side; I straightened it with my shoe and went on into the living-room and the kitchen. I had all the time been trying to steel myself for our meeting, going over the things I would say. I needn't have bothered. The flat was empty.

In the large bedroom the sheets and pillows on the bed lay

smooth and undisturbed. It all looked very much as usual. In the girls' room I found Lucy's bed neat and tidy, and Bonnie's bed unmade—as if she had just got out of it. I stood there, quite still, looking around me, and wondering what it was that was so different about the room. It took me a second before I knew, and when I did, the realisation was like a bucket of cold water in my face.

All Lucy's pictures were gone. There wasn't one left.

Apart from three or four of Bonnie's rather bleak, monochromatic designs, the walls were blank.

And all Lucy's toys and books, too. Everything that was hers I found stuffed away in cupboards and drawers and at the bottom of the big oak chest near the window. The only belongings I could see were Bonnie's. Even her doll was there in view, at last out of its box. Her things were arranged all around the room, taking up as much space as she needed. Not Kate's work. Bonnie's. Just Bonnie's. Just Bonnie being thorough. Bonnie being careful.

Going back down the stairs I found, on the wall above the bottom step, a smear of red. From Bonnie's paintbox, I thought. Bonnie being unusually careless. But this time I was wrong.

EIGHTEEN

I waited half-an-hour and then decided it was time to go.

Before I got back onto the motorway I pulled up near a phone-box to see whether Kate might have returned in the meanwhile. The shop I went into for change displayed a badly written notice saying NO CHANGE GIVEN FOR THE TELEPHONE! SORRY,—and I could see by the pitiless face of the proprietor that it was no joke—except for the *sorry* part which, judging by the cramped lettering, was obviously an afterthought. It took me a couple of tries before I got any twopence pieces; chocolate alone didn't do it so I asked for a packet of Rothmans.

"They'll be in tomorrow," he grudgingly informed me.

"Thanks," I said, "but I won't wait if you don't mind."

He didn't mind, and I ended up with the early edition of an evening paper I didn't want and twenty cigarettes of a brand I didn't like. Afterwards, as I dialled Kate's number, coins poised at the ready, I knew it was all a waste of time. It was. She wasn't back yet.

Later, near the house in Birmingham, I tried to call her again. She still wasn't in. It was disturbing. I couldn't understand it.

Lucy—although perfectly all right in Mrs. Hooper's care—had obviously missed me, and her welcoming hug made me glad and dispelled for a while the uneasiness I felt. It was still only mid-afternoon and, feeling guilty over the fact that I'd had to leave her in the house, I suggested that we go out somewhere.

"Where?" she asked.

"Oh, we'll think of something." I had a sudden brainwave. "If you like we could go swimming." There had to be a pool somewhere in the city.

"Oh, yes!" She took up the idea eagerly. "But I didn't bring my swim-suit."

Even better—we would go shopping first. "We'll get you a new one," I said. "And towels, and trunks for me."

"If we're going to the shops, can I buy a present, as well?"

"Who for?"

"Well—for Mummy. And one for Bonnie."

"Why?"

"Well, be*cause*." She shrugged—it was obvious. "You always buy presents for people when you go on holiday."

*   *   *

After we'd got our swimming-gear Lucy, with financial help from me, bought Kate a bottle of inexpensive perfume. For Bonnie she finally chose a large picture-book. Beside us at the counter a woman was buying a pretty auburn-haired doll. Lucy studied it, pondering for a moment, then finally dismissed it. "No, Bonnie doesn't like dolls."

*   *   *

We had a fine time in the heated, indoor pool. Lucy was a strong swimmer and had no fear at all of the water. She wasn't afraid of heights, either, and took pride in showing off her prowess from the diving-board. We stayed there for nearly two hours, swimming races, chasing each other through the water and generally splashing around. When eventually we came out we felt scrubbed-clean, pleasantly enervated and ravenously hungry.

On the way back I stopped the car near an Indian restaurant —a special treat for her, I hoped—and together we went in and ordered dishes of curried prawns and chicken. As we sat there she asked me again, her face suddenly perturbed: "When shall we be seeing Mummy?" and I answered as before, "Soon, soon," without looking at her; trying to concentrate on the food—suddenly quite tasteless—in front of me.

Just after eight-thirty, when she lay in bed reading, I slipped out of the house and tried once more to get through to Kate. I stood there with the monotonous sound of the ringing tone repeating over and over in my ear long after I knew it wasn't going to be answered.

And Lucy slept restlessly that night. The Indian food had

been a mistake. She woke after midnight and cried peevishly against my shoulder, and I just didn't feel up to the situation. I sat on the edge of her bed and held her in my arms, stroking, soothing. We'd be seeing Mummy soon, yes, of course we would, I assured her. There was no need to worry, we'd be going home soon . . . soon . . . if Mummy didn't come and join us . . . "Don't cry, sweetheart. Don't cry . . ." But she didn't need my soft, comforting words—she needed her mother.

*   *   *

I was late getting up the next morning. On my way back from buying the daily papers I made another attempt to ring Kate. Still no answer. My sense of unease was increasing all the time. Was she playing some kind of game with me? What was she doing? Where had she gone? And why?

After breakfast Lucy and I got into the car and drove away from the house. We found a park and wandered about in the sunshine, breathing in the smell of the grass and trees. The place was swarming with children; all of them seemingly happy. I looked down at Lucy's serious face and said it was a fantastic day, wasn't it? and she answered yes, it was—but her smile was only just there.

I felt so sorry for her. And I asked myself again whether I was doing the right thing. Was my present course of action the only possible one? Wasn't there a less destructive way out? Some other answer to it all . . . ? I wanted to stop, there and then on the pathway, kneel down, put my arms around her and *tell* her—everything—and somehow make her understand that I had seen no alternative. But I couldn't. Of course I couldn't. She must never know. And for the present I would just have to hold on; not give in. *Huh . . . Not give in . . . Hold on . . .* It was all very well to tell myself that—remembering her face as she had clung to me in the night made me wonder how strong I could continue to be.

In the children's area she played, without enthusiasm, on the swings and as I watched her I thought of that *other* time, that *other* park—where Bonnie had tried to kill her. The memory made me thrust aside the pity that was stirring so strongly in me; the pity that had, for a while, threatened to swamp my knowledge of what *was*.

We bought provisions for a cold lunch on the way back to the house. I suggested that perhaps we might return to eat it in the park, but Lucy said no, she'd rather go on to the room. Ugly as it was, it had become, for her, something of a symbol of stability.

Sitting near the window we ate our ham, brown bread and pickles, following it up each with a small apple-pie that came in a neat, clinical little box—the picture on which seemed to have little relation to its contents. I studied her as she sank her small, even teeth into the sugary crust. All this factory-processed food— surely Kate would have managed something better . . .

In the afternoon we went to the cinema. A Walt Disney film was showing—a beckoning finger to the children beginning their holidays—and for the first time that day I sensed Lucy's tightness fade away. I saw excitement touch her as we walked up the steps to the foyer and I blessed Mr. Disney, his dream and his genius.

Sitting side by side in the comparative darkness, Lucy and I watched as Snow White went with her fluid grace from suppression, through terror, to happiness, and I only wished I could have enjoyed it as I should have been able to, as I had done in the past. I wished that I could be like those other fathers who sat there, all of them as spellbound as their children, with no greater concern than that Snow White would be taken in by the story that the poisoned apple was a wishing-apple. Still, I could be glad that Lucy was so completely enraptured. When it was over, and Snow White had been taken off by the prince to her place in the sun, we emerged into our own patch of sunlight in the street outside. Lucy's eyes sparkled and, watching her, I told myself that maybe things weren't as bad as I'd thought. I even found myself whistling—*With A Smile and Song*—as we walked to the car.

I was still whistling when Lucy, looking up from the paper I had bought solely in order to get change for the telephone the day before, said to me in puzzled, rather frightened tones:

"Daddy—"

"Mm?"

"Daddy—this in the paper. It's about Mummy. It says she's in *hospital*."

NINETEEN

"Larkspur Ward, on the fifth floor . . ."

The smiling receptionist waved a hand indicating my path to the right, and I thanked her and moved away, passing doctors, nurses, porters, patients in wheelchairs, and milling visitors carrying magazines, chocolates and flowers. At my side, her coat open, revealing the crisp lemon-yellow of her new dress, Lucy walked quickly, endeavouring to keep up with my long, steady strides. She wasn't complaining, though; she was going to see Mummy, and as eager as I to get there.

At the end of the corridor we stopped and waited a few interminable moments for the lift. Lucy held my hand as we crowded in, her anxiety showing in the pressure of her fingers. In my raincoat pocket the wadded-up newspaper pressed into my side. Ironic, I thought, after all my determination, how everything had been changed by the paper I had hurriedly tossed onto the back seat of the car.

The last hours had passed in a blur of emotions and activity and now, momentarily stilled, I recalled again the fear I had felt when I had seen the small news item about Kate's accident. A small piece, referring to her as ". . . *Kate Robbins, who became so well-known to television viewers for her performance as Marsha in the popular, long-running serial, 'A Quiet Place'* . . ." After so many years away from the public eye she no longer merited more than a couple of paragraphs on the back page. But they had been enough, and Lucy had spotted them. Of Lucy's disappearance with me there had been no mention. It had said nothing of Bonnie's whereabouts, either, though there was no reason why it should. I wondered where Bonnie could be at this moment; who was looking after her . . .

But now the lift doors were opening and Lucy and I were hurrying out, eyeing the signs, finding our way. The ward was divided into separate, open-ended rooms, each one holding no more than four beds. That was good—at least Kate would have some measure of privacy. A nursing sister came towards us and gave an enquiring smile. I told her who I wanted and she looked back and pointed. "You'll find her in there on the right."

"Is it okay if I take my daughter in?"

"I don't see why not." She smiled down at Lucy. "I should think she'll be very happy to see her."

I thanked her and we went on. I had no idea what I would say to Kate, how I should make my approach. But perhaps that wasn't so important. The important thing was that I was setting her tormented mind at rest for a while, relieving her of some of her fears. I was bringing Lucy back to her. I had to. I had no choice. I couldn't let her just lie there, ill and alone. She'd been through enough pain without my adding to it. I'd find another way to deal with the problem of Bonnie, but for the present, while she was out of the way—wherever she might be—she was no threat to Lucy's safety. And I would seek some means to ensure that she never would be in the future.

Then, suddenly, we were there. And I could see Kate over the frosted-glass partition, her head on the pillow, face turned towards the window, hair curling gently on her shoulder. There were other beds, other women lying there, but I hardly noticed them. My chest felt tight and sweat broke out under my arms. I stooped beside Lucy and put my hands on her shoulders.

"Mummy's in there. But I think she's asleep. So we must be quiet when we go in, and not excite her too much." I suppose I was trying to forestall the possibility of any emotional scenes. Lucy nodded quickly, hardly listening, eager to go in. "Yes— yes—" she breathed, and I stood up and held her hand.

"Okay, let's go in."

We moved towards the wide doorway and even as we arrived there Kate turned, saw us and gave a small cry, and the next moment Lucy was at her side, held in the waiting arms, nestling into the well-loved, comforting warmth. Lucy's reception had been predictable—not so my own. I approached quietly, stood awkwardly near the end of the bed and watched as they clung to each other. I saw the tears that sprang into Kate's eyes and Lucy saw them too.

"Oh, don't cry. You'll soon be better. You mustn't be sad."

Kate shook her head. "No, I'm *happy*." The tears streamed down her cheeks.

"Does it hurt much?" Lucy, in fascination, studied the bruises.

"Not now. Not a bit."

The discolouration of Kate's face ran all down one side from her forehead to her jaw. Her left eye was bloodshot and half-closed, while the flesh around it was swollen, dark and angry-looking. I went to the right of the bed, closer to her. She turned and gave me the whisper of a smile, and summoning my courage I put my fingers up to her cheek—but not touching, just a fraction away.

"Poor face . . ." I said.

She shook her head.

"It doesn't matter now."

We fell silent. After a while I said:

"What happened? The paper said you'd had a fall."

"Downstairs. On Friday night."

"You slipped?"

"I can't really remember. I tripped or something. I don't remember much about it. I was upstairs sorting out some clothes and stuff. Bonnie was asleep in her room. I came out and started down the stairs and—*pow*—that was it."

"How did you get here?"

"Mrs. Taverner. She called the ambulance."

"Thank heaven for Mrs. Taverner."

"Yes."

"Has she been in to see you?"

"She's away. Taken the children to the seaside for a week. She left yesterday morning . . . and took Bonnie with her."

The silence fell again. I nodded mechanically. Kate said after a moment:

"But Mr. Taverner's been in. He brought me a note from his wife." She indicated an envelope on the bedside table. I didn't pick it up; I stood looking down at her, at the ugly colouring of

her cheek, remembering the smear of blood on the wall that I
had taken to be paint.

Stooping, I gently kissed her bruised lips, and she reached up
and held on to me. I hovered awkwardly over the bed, only just
on balance, and still she held on, saying nothing, her hands at
the back of my neck. My eyes were shut tight, squeezing back
the tears that threatened.

After a while I sat down on the chair at her side and held her
hand. She put her other arm around Lucy, hugging her close.

"I knew," she said at last, "that if I waited long enough you'd
bring her back."

"I'm sorry . . ."

"I knew you would."

"Forgive me, Kate. Forgive me, please."

"Yes. Yes . . ."

I whispered suddenly:

"I want us to be as we once were. You don't know how much
I want it."

She closed her eyes for a moment, nodded.

"Yes, I want it, too."

*   *   *

Although we stayed for another half-hour or more, we had no
real opportunity to talk—not about things that mattered. There
were some visitors with the other patients in the room and it was
obvious from one or two glances our way that Kate was something of a special attraction. Also, her tearful greeting, plus the
fact that I had not come to see her before, was probably extra
cause for their added interest; how she had explained away my
absence I had no idea—if she had. So we were forced to talk of
minor matters, while all the things I really wanted to say I had
to keep to myself.

Lucy was in no way inhibited, though, and was full of her
own stories that covered the silences that fell between Kate and
me. She kept coming in relating odd bits of the adventure she
had had, telling of the house in Birmingham, the restaurant

meals, the swimming, *Snow White* and, finally, with some pride, how *she* had been the one to find in the paper the news of Kate's accident. I looked at her animated, happy face, listened to her bubbling chatter and thought of how she had often been over the past days. Now, in the telling, she imbued the adventure with an air of excitement and joy—which had not been present when it was actually happening. I don't know what Kate's thoughts were as she nodded her interest and made the appropriate comments to Lucy's narrative. I could see no resentment in her eyes. She smiled warmly; "Really?" "Did you now?" "Aren't you a lucky girl . . . ?"

The other visitors were leaving. It was just past eight. Our allotted time was over. As I got up and beckoned to Lucy a little look of fear flicked across Kate's face. I said at once, "We'll be in to see you tomorrow afternoon," and the look went and she smiled her relief.

"Good, I won't be going anywhere."

I grinned at the welcome humour. "Anyway, not long and you'll be back home for good."

We kissed her then, and left. As we turned the corner into the corridor I looked back and saw her smile and wave. That smile, a little painful in appearance, but there, very much there. Keep hold of it, I told myself, it's your only hope for the future.

A few yards down the corridor I saw the nursing sister in conversation with a white-coated man. She gave me a nod of recognition then turned back to him. As I approached he stepped towards me—a man of my own age, eager and immaculate with a smile that belonged to somebody much younger.

"Mr. Marlowe—? How do you do. I'm Doctor Geller."

We shook hands. He smiled down at Lucy then consciously lowered his voice slightly.

"Your wife must have been very happy to see you. She's been very anxious. I'm so glad you were able to get back."

I nodded. I didn't know where I was supposed to have been, or what I was supposed to have been doing there. "Yes," I said.

"She had a very bad fall. Very nasty."

"Yes . . . How long will she be here? She's hoping she can go home soon. She was talking about tomorrow."

He shook his head. "Well, no. But possibly in three or four days. Have to see how she is. She's been under severe shock. We mustn't take any chances."

"No . . ."

There was a pause. He said sympathetically:

"Naturally she's upset and depressed, though she'll get over it all right. But she'll need your help in the meantime."

"Yes."

"She's young enough, however, and there's no reason why, in another year, you can't try again."

"Yes . . . I understand . . ." I wasn't sure that I did. I stared at him while it sank in, and he looked at me. He must have seen the realisation in my eyes.

"I'm sorry," he said. "I really am very sorry about the baby."

I heard myself say: "Yes. Yes." I was like a parrot. "Yes. Yes, thank you . . ."

And then I was telling Lucy, "Stay there for a minute," then turning and almost running the few yards back along to the ward where Kate lay. She looked up in astonishment as I entered and went to her bedside. Without giving her any chance to talk at all, I clasped her hand in mine and whispered urgently:

"I didn't know. Darling, I didn't know. Believe me. Why didn't you tell me?"

"Tell you—? About—about the baby?"

"Yes. You should have told me."

"I was going to. That day—"

"God, you should have told me."

"There was no chance afterwards. You were gone. I only had Bonnie."

Bonnie . . .

I had to know. I had to ask it:

"Did you say anything? To her?"

I kept my face impassive as she answered:

"Oh, yes. Bonnie knew. I told her on the day you left."

*   *   *

It began to rain as Lucy and I drove home, quite heavily, and we made a dash from the car for the front entrance. I wasn't only anxious to get out of the wet, though—it was imperative that I get in touch with Mrs. Taverner and I just prayed her husband was at home. As soon as Lucy and I got indoors and took our coats off I left her and went across the landing and knocked on the Taverners' door. I had a great sense of relief when I heard sounds of movement coming from the other side. Thank God. Then, a moment later Mr. Taverner was opening the door, standing there buttoning his shirt, getting ready to leave for work. I'd caught him only just in time.

"Ah," he said, "you're back. Good!" giving me a broad smile that deepened the creases in his lean, angular face. Whether he knew why I had gone I had no idea, but if he did he wasn't holding it against me.

"I've just been to see my wife . . ."

He nodded and ran a hand through his thinning hair. "Poor girl. How is she today?"

"Much better, thanks. I'm very grateful that you went to visit her . . ."

"Oh, no, don't mention it. I wish I could have been some real help."

"You were. Believe me. And Mrs. Taverner." I hesitated. "I'm told she took Bonnie away with her and the children."

"Well, it seemed the best thing to do under the circumstances. She couldn't just leave her here on her own. She was taking the kids off, anyway, so it seemed the logical thing to do. At least the little thing would be with people she knew." He grinned. "She's probably having a right old time—I wouldn't be surprised." He turned and looked over towards the window where the rain pelted against the panes. "Though I wouldn't guarantee that it'll continue if this keeps up very long."

"Where did they go?"

"Of course, you'll be wanting Bonnie back again. Though she'll be fine where she is for a few days, I'm sure. Anyway, I'll get you the phone number and address. They're with her brother in Bournemouth. Come on in."

He turned and I followed him into the untidy living-room and watched while he searched in the muddle for pencil and paper. "Rather them than me," he said as he wrote. "I can't stand Bournemouth and I can't stand her brother. Still, it takes all sorts—so they tell me." I didn't ask what particular sort Mrs. Taverner's brother was, but thanked him and took the scrap of paper he held out in his broad hand.

"I'll phone her now." I was moving to the door. "I'll give her your love when I do."

"Yes." He spoke as if the thought hadn't occurred to him. "Yes, do that, please."

Back in the flat, Lucy greeted me with the information that she was hungry. I realised I was as well. It had been hours since we'd eaten.

"Okay, sweetheart," I reassured her, "we'll have something in a minute." I could open some tins or we could go out. But for the moment food wasn't the upper-most thing in my mind. "I've got to make a phone call first. Just be patient for a while."

It was the brother who answered the phone. "I'll get her," he said, and after half-a-minute Mrs. Taverner's familiar voice came on the line. After she had enquired about Kate's progress and various predictable phrases had passed between us I asked how Bonnie was getting on.

"Oh, she's enjoying herself immensely. Having a wonderful time."

"That's—marvellous. When do you plan to return?"

"Anxious to see her, are you? Well, not till Saturday afternoon. But you'll let her stay till then, won't you?"

"Oh, yes," I said quickly. "It's very good of you to look after her. Believe me, she's much better off with you as things are right now—if she's no trouble."

"Trouble? That little love? No trouble at all."

"You're very kind, Mrs. Taverner. Really." I meant it. "And I can't tell you how grateful I am that you helped Kate as you did."

"I only did what anyone else would have done under the circumstances. I wish I could have done more."

"Do you know what happened exactly?"

"The accident? Well, the first thing I knew about it was when Bonnie came ringing at our bell. It must have been just after ten o'clock that night. I suppose she'd heard her mother fall—noise must have woken her up. Thank the Lord she had the sense to come and get me. Such a clever little girl—such presence of mind. She said her mother had fallen down. So, of course I went in straight-away. Your wife was lying at the bottom of the stairs. She must have had a terrible bump. She was right out. I think those stairs are too steep. I've always thought it about ours. They *seem* steep and—"

"What happened then?" I cut in. "You phoned the ambulance—"

"Yes—after I'd put a couple of cushions under her head. The ambulance got there in no time. They were fantastic. She'd come round by the time they arrived, but she was in an awful state, she really was. I told her not to worry about Bonnie—said I'd take care of her. There wasn't really much else I could do. So Bonnie slept in with Gillian that night and then yesterday—next morning—as you weren't there, I thought the best thing to do was to bring her away with my lot. Well, rather than have her go to some strangers—which is what would have happened." She paused. "Dave phoned me yesterday afternoon when he'd been to the hospital . . ." Another slight pause. "The doctor told him about . . . well . . . the baby . . . And I'm really sorry. I really am . . ."

"Thank you . . ."

"Anyway, the main thing is, she's getting better. And you tell her she's not to worry about Bonnie at all. She'll be quite safe and well looked-after."

"I will. Thank you." *God bless you, Mrs. Taverner, for taking Bonnie away. It gives me a week. In a week I could do a lot. Perhaps I can make sure that she never comes back.*

I had one more question.

"Do you know how Kate came to fall? She doesn't know . . ."

"Oh, well, I think it must have been little Bonnie. She'd been playing on the stairs, I expect."

"—I'm not sure what you mean . . ."

"Well, you know how children are with their toys—leave them anywhere . . . I should think your wife must have slipped on it."

"There was something left there?"

"Yes—lying on the stairs. Later she put it back in her room, but it was on the stairs when I went in."

"What? What was it?"

"Oh, I thought I *said* . . . It was Bonnie's doll."

TWENTY

"**I** must ask you, Mr. Marlowe, whether you've really thought this out. Are you sure this is what you want?"

"Absolutely." My fingers drummed on my knee, betraying my nervousness. I stilled them. The face of the social worker, Mrs. Warner, who sat looking at me across the large desk showed consternation. I was a problem, and her distress was evident in the way she put up her hand and smoothed her already smooth, greying hair.

"But she's not a foster-child, Mr. Marlowe. We could—would —take her into care at once if she *were*—if there was any kind of trouble. But she's yours. She's your daughter. Legally adopted."

"I know that. But you've got to do something." I consciously put a hardness into my voice—which she didn't react to. She just looked at the pad on which she'd been making notes.

"You say she's nearly four."

"Yes. In August."

"And your other daughter—how old is she?"

"Just ten."

She paused, choosing her words. "This is a very big step you're taking, you realise. Is the situation really so—impossible?"

"Yes. We just can't cope with her any more."

"She's unmanageable?"

"You could say that . . ."

"And does your wife feel as strongly as you?"

"My wife is ill and under a great deal of strain. She's very recently had a miscarriage . . ."

I knew I shouldn't have said that. The woman would think that *that* was what had precipitated my demands—that they were the results of temporary worry and neurosis.

"I'm very sorry to hear that. And of course she's under a strain. But perhaps she'll feel differently about it in a while— once she's feeling better . . ."

"I know how *I* feel," I said, too quickly. "I want the child gone."

"And does your wife want the child gone as much as you do?"

I hesitated for a second. "—Yes."

"There are many times, Mr. Marlowe, I know," she smiled, her voice taking on a sympathetic tone, "when a child can be a bit of a problem, and they *can* get you down—I know how it is. But mostly it's never *that* serious. Families go through their problems—they have setbacks—but they do *get through* them. Don't you think—" here she leaned forward slightly, "—that you're possibly over-reacting a bit? You might merely be going through a little rough patch. It happens to all of us from time to time . . ."

She was doing her best, I knew it, but only one thing would satisfy me. "I want her taken away," I said shortly. "I want you to take her into care. Anywhere—it doesn't matter where—just so long as she leaves my home."

Silence for a few seconds.

"She really is a—a bad influence?"

"She's evil."

It was too strong a word, and the woman's eyebrows lifted slightly. I must be coming over as a complete madman. "Yes," I said, nodding, "she's a bad influence." Bonnie had murdered my three sons, tried to kill my daughter, made me sterile and caused my wife to have a miscarriage, and I had to describe her as "a bad influence". I said again,

"Somebody's got to come and take her away. *Soon.*"

"Well, now even if it's seen as the best course it can't be done just like that. We have to look into the situation first. You must remember that a child's happiness is at stake here."

And Lucy's life was at stake too. "Soon," I said firmly. "It must be arranged before the end of the week." I wanted to hand Bonnie over as soon as she returned.

"Well," she looked at her notes again, "I think the best thing is for me or one of my colleagues to come and see you and your wife in your home—providing she's well enough. We can see the child too, then, and discuss the whole thing properly."

"I told you—my wife is ill. I don't want her bothered."

"But you must realise that both parents have to agree to such a step. We have to have the approval of both parents. We always insist on meeting all the relatives."

I'd never imagined it would be so difficult. "Can't you understand?" I said, "I just want that child gone. If I have to I'll come and dump her here in your office!"

She looked at me steadily for a second before replying.

"If you are that desperate and did take such a step then we'd be forced to take her into temporary care. But you must know that it would only be temporary. Your wife could reclaim her immediately." She paused. "—If your wife wants the child."

If your wife wants the child . . . It was becoming a farce. I got up and moved towards the door. When I turned and looked back the woman was standing, watching me, her hands spread on the desk before her. She said kindly:

"You're obviously very upset. I think we should all sit down and talk this thing over. I'm sure with a little help—counselling —we can do something . . ."

Help, counselling—they wouldn't help where Bonnie was concerned. "Thank you," I said wearily. "It doesn't matter any more. I'm sorry I wasted your time."

*　　*　　*

It was still raining that afternoon when Lucy and I went to visit Kate again. I saw Doctor Geller in the corridor and he told me how pleased he was with her progress, adding that he thought she'd be well enough to leave on Wednesday, providing there were no setbacks.

I could see the difference in her too. Her face lit up as we approached. Her hair was newly-brushed and shining and she looked brighter, rested and relaxed.

"The doctor says you can come home on Wednesday," I said when I had kissed her.

"I feel well enough to go home now."

"Well, you'll just have to grin and bear it. Anyway, you need the rest, I'm sure."

We stayed there for nearly two hours. Just before we got ready to leave I said:

"I talked to Mrs. Taverner on the phone."

"—How is Bonnie?"

"She's fine. They'll be coming back on Saturday. You just think about getting better. That's the important thing."

*   *   *

I don't know the precise moment when the idea of killing Bonnie came into my head. Perhaps it had been there for a long time, below my awareness, only surfacing now when everything else had failed. Any plans I had had for getting rid of her by lawful means had been scotched by my interview with the social worker, and I'd been left exactly where I'd started. Now, by the weekend, Bonnie would have returned to the fold, and from that moment Lucy's life would be in the greatest danger.

I had only to stand in the room which had been stripped of Lucy's belongings to know the singleness of Bonnie's purpose. It came through so clearly. She would never rest until everything—the room, Kate's love and caring—was permanently hers, and hers alone.

Yet I couldn't take Lucy away again. It hadn't worked before and it wouldn't work a second time. I couldn't separate her for ever from her mother, and any temporary flight would only put the danger off till a later time. When she returned Bonnie would still be here, waiting.

Really, simply, I was presented with a choice, and if the choice was between Bonnie's life and Lucy's life then I *had* no choice. None at all. I thought briefly of what might happen to *me* as a result, but I wasn't that concerned—I just didn't care any more. I had lost my three sons, and my marriage would certainly be gone for ever whatever the outcome. I had nothing left to lose—nothing that I cared about—only Lucy. Years in prison?

—the prospect meant nothing—a small price to pay if it would buy for Lucy her life.

I spread out my hands before me, turned them over, studied them. They were hands that had been used only to build things —no earth-shattering things, nothing likely to become a part of history, but still, creations for all that. I wondered how I could turn them to destruction. Then when I looked back again to the near-bare walls, to Bonnie's doll over on the chest, I knew that I must.

While Lucy was safely out of earshot, soaking in her bath, I phoned Mrs. Taverner. My call was brief. I told her I'd try to be in Bournemouth to collect Bonnie on Friday morning.

"You can't wait till I bring her back on Saturday . . . ?"

I'd gone over it in my mind—carefully: Saturday would be too late and Thursday—Kate's first day home—would be too early; it might not be easy for me to get away.

"No," I said, "Friday. But please—don't mention it to Kate if she phones you—I'd like it to be a surprise."

*　　*　　*

On our visit to Kate in the afternoon I took with me a case containing the clothes she'd asked for—her blouse and skirt, coat, shoes, etc.

"They've been so kind to me here," she said, "but I can't wait to get home tomorrow." She looked brighter than ever now. The bruise on her face had faded a little more and the promise of leaving the next day had given her an added lift. In view of what I was planning to do I knew the period of happiness didn't have that long to run.

*　　*　　*

The next morning there came from my publishers an advance copy of a book I'd illustrated—Hans Andersen's *The Little Mermaid*—and after a late breakfast Lucy and I sat together on the sofa and turned over the crisp new pages. I was pleased with the book; they'd used a good-quality paper and my pictures had been carefully and faithfully reproduced. Lucy fell in love with it right away, and twenty minutes later while I was busy with the carpet-sweeper—getting the place in order for Kate's return—she was still poring over it.

"I wish it were Monday tomorrow," she said.

"Why?"

"I want to take this book to school, to show my friend, Carol. She thinks you're fantastic. She said she wishes *her* dad could draw."

I stopped working and looked at her. She had gone back to be absorbed in the book again but the happiness with which she had spoken still showed in a small, lingering smile on her face. I turned away from the look, went over to the window, stood gazing out.

Yes, I could kill Bonnie. And by doing so I could save Lucy's life. I had thought it all through—right to the outcome, sure that what happened to me afterwards would not matter; I could face the years in prison, the permanent separation from Lucy and Kate, because I would have done what needed to be done—and if I *couldn't* face it then it didn't matter much either. But in planning the means of giving Lucy back her life I had not envisaged the *quality* of her life. Was that little smile of pride and love to be replaced by disillusionment, fear, shame and mistrust—? Yes, it would be. And for how long—? —Always? Yes . . . She would grow up with the certain knowledge that I had cold-bloodedly murdered her younger sister. I could never give to her such a legacy.

And Kate, too. Added to her grief she would now live with hatred—where she had known only love.

My thoughts were racing and into my mind came the memory of a particular stretch of road I had taken once not too far from Bournemouth. The hillside fell away on one side in a steep, breath-catching drop—the view was clear before my eyes, fixed like a picture-postcard. I stood trembling, suddenly seeing in my mind's eye the bonnet of the car as it plunged over the grass verge, smashing through the flimsy barrier of the hedge—and then down, down to certain blackness—blankness—and the ending.

I had told Mrs. Taverner that I'd collect Bonnie on Friday. I still would. And that's when it must happen—an *accident*. But not only to Bonnie. When Bonnie went, I would go with her.

* * *

Lucy and I drove to the hospital to find Kate all ready, dressed and waiting for us—she had been, she said, for well over an hour. It was a miserable day, raining heavily again, but she wasn't daunted by the wet. We stopped at a supermarket on the way back and the three of us walked between the banks of shelves while she filled the trolley-basket to restock the larder. I could see she was still nervous to a degree, so it was probably good for her to be occupied with normal, everyday tasks. She hadn't mentioned the loss of the baby since the time the doctor had told me about it, but I was sure it must still be there, very much on her mind.

And that night she lay beside me in bed and wept on my shoulder.

"I wanted him so much," she cried. "God, I wanted him so much . . ."

I let her cry. There were so many tears inside her waiting to be shed.

Long after she was still and sleeping, warm against me, I lay awake thinking over what was to come. I realised that I would have to tell her—sometime—of my decision to go and collect Bonnie—otherwise she would never believe in the subsequent "accident". But I could manage it all right. I could be sufficiently convincing and make her believe that my attitude towards Bonnie had changed—that I had come to my senses. She was *eager* to believe it and she *would* believe.

* * *

After breakfast the next morning, Thursday, I got ready to go to the studio. Really it was Kate's idea. She was well enough, she insisted, to do a few jobs that had to be done around the flat, and she was eager to get back to her routine. Lucy would be there too, so she'd be perfectly all right.

In a way I was rather relieved to be going; it wasn't easy to face her rather strained contentment and determined attempts to show that everything was going to be okay. Besides, there was work that *I* should be getting on with, work that had already been delayed for several days and was still sitting in the boot of the car—not that I felt at all like doing it.

As I stood in the hall putting on my raincoat, she came out to me, watched me in silence. I nodded towards the rain-patterned window and smiled, muttering about the "bloody weather", and she came closer, reached up and pulled the collar of my coat up around my ears.

"Don't be too late back," she said.

"No, I won't. And don't you overdo it."

"I'll be fine . . ."

We faced each other, smiling. To an outsider everything would have looked as usual—but in reality nothing was.

"I should have told you about the baby earlier," she said.

"—It's over now."

"Yes."

A pause, then she said haltingly, trying to read in my eyes the reaction to her words:

"But it—it doesn't have to be—so—so final . . ."

I said nothing. She went on:

"The doctor told me—well—I can still have another child—we can still have another. Just because—this happened—is no reason why we can't . . ." She looked away. "He said it's no reason," she finished lamely.

I put my arms around her, held her to me and kissed her, my mouth gently brushing the mark of the bruise.

"No reason at all," I lied, "if that's what you want."

*   *   *

When I got to my room I unpacked the stuff from the car and tried to settle down to do something, but it was almost impossible—I felt that practically each pencil stroke required a conscious effort. In the end I gave up.

It had been on my mind since leaving the flat that there was nothing to stop me going to collect Bonnie *this* morning—I was free to do so—and I sat there in a sweat, trying to come to a decision, telling myself that it had to be done and trembling with fear at the prospect of it.

After nearly two hours of deliberating, sitting over my forgotten drawing-board, I made up my mind: if it had to be done then it was as well to get it over with quickly; Macbeth and his wife had been faced with a similar problem and come up with the same resolution.

Taking a very deep breath I picked up the phone and dialled the Bournemouth number.

There was no answer. And they could be out anywhere—and who knew when they'd be back? So it would have to be tomorrow after all. As I put the phone down my heart hammered with relief at my temporary reprieve.

I went to a local pub for an early lunch but found I could eat hardly anything. It didn't matter. I sat there with my beer while the time passed and the rain beat against the windows—would it never stop? I stayed till closing-time. When I got back to the front door of the house I found Kate waiting for me, sheltering in the narrow porch.

"Kate . . ."

The smile I started to give her died on my face; I could see by her mouth and steady eyes that something was wrong.

"Well," she asked, "have we got to stand out here looking at each other?"

I unlocked the door and stepped aside to let her pass. She went by me and, without looking back, started up the stairs. When we got inside my room she turned and faced me.

"How did you get here?" I asked.

"A taxi." Her voice was clipped. She had a slightly wild look about her. The rain had darkened the shoulders of her light raincoat and wisps of hair clung damply to her forehead. "What brings you out in this weather?" I asked. "You should be at home. You're not well enough to be out yet."

"I'm all right."

"Do you want to sit down?" I indicated a chair.

"No. I don't intend staying very long."

"Kate, what is it? What's the matter?"

She shrugged. "I should have thought it was obvious. I wanted to see you."

"Couldn't it have waited till I got back?"

"No. I had to see you now. That's why I've been standing out there."

I waited for her to continue. At last she said:

"I'm going to divorce you."

"—I see."

"That's all you can say—'I see'." She shook her head. "I don't trust you, Alan. I'll never trust you or believe you again. I don't want ever to live with you again. I want you to—pack up everything that's yours and leave. Find somewhere else to live." Her face was drained of colour and against the whiteness the bruise showed livid.

"Would you tell me why you're saying all this?" I asked. I was trying to appear calm.

"Yes, I'll tell you!" she blurted out. "A certain Mrs. Warner came to see me!"

"Mrs. Warner—? I don't know any Mrs. Warner."

"That's surprising, considering you went to see her. She's a *social worker*. She works in the Adoptions Section of the Social Services Department!"

Sweet Jesus, why did that have to happen?

I said weakly:

"Oh . . . yes . . ."

"Oh, yes," she echoed. "Now you remember. Good. Well, you'll be interested to know that she came round to—to discuss the case of our daughter, Bonnie." She almost spat the next words at me: "You asked them to take her away. Ever since you got back you've been so—so *nice*—so cons*i*derate—and all the time you've just been *plotting*—trying to arrange for Bonnie to be taken away! How could you do it? Why?"

Suddenly I could taste the beer in my mouth. I felt sick. I turned away. *"You know* why."

"I know you think *you* know why."

"Listen!" I spun, grabbed her by the shoulders and held her. "Listen to me—!"

"Let me go."

"Listen! God damn it! You're going to listen! I won't stand by and let that—that—creature destroy—*everything*—just because you're—blinded by your maternal feelings! She killed our sons. She made me sterile. *Yes!*" I almost shouted at the surprise that came into her eyes. "It's *true!* She didn't want us to have any more children, and eventually she made sure of it. So she gave me mumps. It was no accident."

"No, no, no—" Kate shook her head from side to side. "You hate her so—that's why you're saying all this."

"Yes, and I've got good reason to hate her. You want to hear more? She caused your miscarriage. It was her doll you slipped on, going down the stairs. That doll she never *ever* played with. 'Bonnie was in bed asleep'—isn't that what you told me? No— Bonnie *wasn't* in bed asleep. Bonnie was in bed waiting her chance. She'd accomplished everything she wanted—the boys were gone—I couldn't possibly give you another child—and I'd taken Lucy away. She had the nest all to herself. And then you go and tell her you're pregnant." I dropped my hands back to my sides. She stayed there—staring at me, wide-eyed.

"If you hadn't told her," I went on, "that baby you wanted would still be safe inside you. That was your mistake. And that night while you were—what?—sorting out clothes, I think you said—she crept out of her room and put her doll on one of the top steps. Then went and got back into bed. You, turning the corner from the landing, didn't see the doll—and that was it. You went down. She took a chance, mind you—you could have been more seriously hurt—but I suppose she must have been desperate. And if the fall hadn't been serious enough she would have done something else in the next day or two. You can be sure of that—"

What was the point? I was hitting my head against a brick

wall. Suddenly I just didn't care whether she saw the truth or not. I turned away. I should have driven to Bournemouth today —and that would have been the end of it.

The room was silent except for the swish of tyres on the wet road below. Into the quiet Kate said softly, her voice full of horror and wonder:

"Such a terrible thing can't be possible . . ."

"Yes."

"But *how?*"

"Don't ask me how. I only know it is."

"Oh, God . . ."

I thought I had detected a note of—nothing approaching *belief*, but something else—a softening of her resistance? I looked at her. No. If her belief had wavered it had only been for a moment. She was glaring back at me, as immovable as ever.

"You don't know that child at all," I said.

"*You* don't know her! She's gentle and sweet and loving!"

"She's very, very *clever*—and quite ruthless."

"You should have seen her while you were away. You never saw a more affectionate child."

"Of course! Can't you understand? It wasn't because *I* was away—it was because *Lucy* was away. Lucy was *gone* and that's what Bonnie *wanted*."

"It's *impossible* to make you understand," she said, moving away. "I've told you what I came here to tell you—and that's it." In the doorway she turned. "For an artist you're unbelievably blind. You're a slave to your outsize imagination—I know that now. Well, *I'm not. I know. I* can *see* what goes on. I *know love* when I see it."

"All right, Kate." I wanted her to go. I wouldn't wait—*couldn't* wait till tomorrow, I'd decided—I'd drive to Bournemouth as soon as she'd gone. But she hadn't finished—she kept hammering away. "You don't open your eyes. You're determined to see only what you want to see—"

I nodded, I wasn't even looking at her. The time, precious time, was ticking away. *Go away, Kate. Please go.*

"You should have seen them—how happy they were to see each other again—"

". . . What . . . ?"

"So—fond of each other . . ."

I whirled to face her.

"What do you mean—? Are you saying that Bonnie's *back?*"

"Yes."

"That can't be . . . Mrs. Taverner told me they'd be coming back on *Saturday.*"

"Well, they're back now. They left early because of the rain. What's all this about? Why are you—?"

"Where are they now?"

"Who?"

"Lucy and Bonnie, of course! Where are they?"

"At home! Where else would they be!"

"You've left them *alone? Together?*"

"*What's wrong with you?*" she shrieked at me. "I came here to tell you that—"

"The girls—" I shouted back at her. "You don't know what you've done!" I spun on the carpet, aimless in my blind panic.

"They're all right. Perfectly. And Mrs. Taverner said she'd pop in and check on them."

"Knowing Bonnie," I flung at her, "that is *no comfort!*" Then I was moving across the room, reaching out for the telephone.

TWENTY ONE

The dial of the telephone revolved at an incredibly slow speed. *Hurry up! Hurry up!* I urged—the wait was endless. But at last I heard the ringing tone and then, a few seconds later, Lucy's voice.

"Hello—?"

"Lucy—?"

"Yes." She recognised my voice at once. "Hello, Daddy."

The relief I felt made my voice shake as I asked:

"Are you all right?"

She didn't answer, and then, into the silence Kate was grabbing at my arm, starting to speak. Impatiently I shook her off.

"Lucy, are you all right?" I repeated.

"I . . . I think so . . ."

"What do you mean—you think so?"

"Well, it's . . . it's Bonnie . . ." Her voice was small over the wire, small and scared. My heart began to thump. I said, trying to sound off-hand:

"What about her?"

"She . . . Well, she's being so . . . *funny* . . ."

"In what way?"

"Well, she won't leave me alone. She keeps following me. All the time."

"Perhaps she just wants to play—that's all . . ." I didn't believe it myself—not for a moment. And Lucy didn't believe it either.

"—No. It's not like when she plays. It's . . . different. She looks at me like—even *now*—she's looking at me so . . . strangely . . ." The fear was stronger now in her voice. "Daddy . . . I'm afraid."

I thought I could choke on the tightness of my breathing. "Darling—" I began, but Kate leaned over and wrenched the receiver from my hand. "All this nonsense!" she said. "Let me talk to her—" Without hesitating I snatched the phone back again, not caring that my nail dug into her chin, drawing a trace of blood.

"Listen, my dear," I said into the mouthpiece. "I'll tell you what I want you to do. I want you to go out of the flat and ring Mrs. Taverner's bell. Keep ringing until she lets you in. Then stay with her until I get home. All right?"

"I can't . . ."

"Why? Why can't you?"

"The door's locked—the big lock—not the other one."

"What!" I turned to Kate. "Did you lock them in together?"

Fingers to the small wound on her chin she looked away, ignoring me. I half-grabbed, half-hit her shoulder so hard that she lurched, almost falling. I gripped the lapel of her coat.

"*Answer me!* Did you lock them in?"

"Of course not." She tore herself away. "Don't be stupid."

"Well, they're locked in *now*. Where did you leave the key?"

"It's kept where it's always kept—on the shelf by the clock! But you *know* that lock's never used during the day."

I went back to the phone.

"Listen, Lucy . . ."

"Yes, Daddy . . ."

"The key is on the shelf by the clock. Have you ever used the big key before?"

"No."

"Well, you'll manage all right. Turn it towards the window. But you'll need to press hard. You understand?"

"Yes . . ."

"Good girl. Now just don't hang up the phone, but just go and get the key and do as I tell you. And don't worry. Okay?"

"Okay."

"That's my girl . . ."

I heard the rattle of the receiver as she laid it down on the table. Seconds went by. Kate said:

"What's happening? Would you mind telling me what this is all about?"

I ignored her; I was listening for Lucy's return. After a few moments her voice was there on the line again.

"Daddy?"

"Did you get the key?"

"It's not there."

Christ. "It *must* be," I said. "Did you look properly?"

"Yes. It's gone."

"Are you sure?"

"Yes."

"All right, baby, it doesn't matter." I paused, dumb, not knowing what to tell her—*anything* that would keep her safe until I could get there. "Listen," I said, "Mummy and I are on our way home right now," I was reaching for my car keys as I spoke. "Until I'm there I don't want you to play with Bonnie at all. Don't go near her. You understand?"

"Yes."

"Good." I turned to Kate. "I know there's no lock on our bedroom door, but can the girls' room be locked from the inside?"

"Yes—but why?"

"How does it lock—?"

"There's a key in a jar by the window . . ."

"Lucy—" I said quickly. "—If you go up to your—" Then I stopped. The phone at the other end had gone quite dead. When I dialled again the ringing tone just went on and on—and I knew it wasn't going to be answered.

Slamming down the receiver I hurried to the door. "Quick!" I said to Kate over my shoulder, "we've got to hurry!" Maddeningly slow behind me, she protested, and I turned back to her, making no effort to hide my fury and my fear, my words hissing out through gritted teeth.

"Listen! Either come with me now, and fast, or stay here! I don't give a damn! All I care about is *Lucy!*" Then I turned, ran down the stairs and out onto the pavement. When I got to my car in the next street I looked back and saw Kate just coming round the corner, running. I got in, switched on the ignition and swung open the door for her.

"Hurry!"

She got in beside me, and I revved the motor and moved the car out to join the flow of traffic.

It was a nightmare ride.

Looking back, I see myself hunched up over the wheel, Kate pale and silent at my side. It seemed that all the other vehicles on the road were bent on hindering our progress, and I could only retaliate with muttered curses and invective.

At last, after twenty-five minutes, six red lights, and a near-thing with a U-turning taxi, we got there.

Less than a hundred yards from the flats I saw an empty parking-space; I drove in, switched off and jumped out and, with Kate hurrying, just yards behind me, ran along the street. Turning the corner I looked up towards our flat. And relief poured over me, making me cry out into the air.

There, high above at the living-room window, Lucy was looking down to the street.

Thank God! Thank God!

She saw me, and a look of joy came over her face. I slowed, smiled, waved to her, and saw her urgently wave back. I was just about to hurry on again when I saw that she was starting to open the window. A man coming towards us looked at me in surprise as I shouted up:

"NO! NO! *Don't open the window! Lucy, don't!*"

Perhaps she didn't hear me; perhaps she was just too relieved to see us there, but she did open the window, wide, looking down at Kate and me, and saying something which I couldn't hear, gesticulating wildly.

"Go back inside!" I yelled.

It looked to me then as if she started to withdraw into the room—for a moment she was gone from my sight. But it was only for a moment. She reappeared almost immediately, her head turned away as if seeing something—or someone—just behind her. For another split-second she remained there, and then, her white face frozen in a mask of fear, she turned in full view again. She seemed to be leaning out—out—lower, lower still, fingers scrabbling on the window-frame. "NO!" I cried, "NO!" and saw her mouth open wide as she screamed in terror.

For one brief instant I thought I glimpsed the top of a corn-coloured head. Then the next instant her hands had lost their frantic hold and she was falling out, over the sill, plunging downward into space.

*   *   *

The seconds that followed straight afterwards are blurred in my memory. There was her scream, the sound of the impact on the concrete and then Kate's cry as she ran forward. I hear other voices, see other faces as they gather quickly around, all filling the afternoon with their noises of horror. Kate throws herself down—in the rain and the blood—across Lucy's body, as if to protect her from further hurt—her mouth opening like a puppet's in dry, silent screams. I can feel my heart beat faster, faster as I turn away and run up the stairs to the third floor.

The blur is gone then; from that moment everything remains clear.

The door to the flat is *unlocked*. The key is there on the shelf, right next to the clock—where it always is. Beside the telephone with its useless, dangling flex, stands Bonnie—looking at me with wide, innocent eyes. The hate inside me is like an explosion.

I move forward, and speak.

"I'm going to kill you."

I remember how my hands reached out, taking her by the throat, pressing—such a little neck; such a little girl; and it should have been so easy. But she fought—God, how she fought me!—with the strength of someone twice her size.

With a power and agility that took me completely by surprise, she swung in, kicking at me, her little Mickey Mouse shoes viciously lashing out at my crotch. I dodged the first blow and her foot only grazed my hip, but her next aim was deadly and I doubled-up, gasping, falling to the floor. Yet I held on, still, dragging her with me. And I wasn't going to let go until she was dead.

She struggled like a wild thing, something not human; her limbs were everywhere, and she writhed and twisted in my grasp as slippery as a reptile. Digging her finger-nails deep into my flesh she wrenched her head away and brought her teeth down hard on my right hand, ferociously biting, biting, till I could feel the bone giving way. Pain was shooting all up my arm, and I cried out and swung my left fist at her temple with all the strength I could find. She reeled back, flat, from the blow, and I scrambled forward and threw the weight of my body heavily on top of her, pinning her there, taking her by the throat again and squeezing, squeezing . . .

And then other hands were there, clutching at me, pulling at my arms, dragging me away. I see the look on Mr. Taverner's face as he looms above me—but hazy, through the cloud of pain and madness that is all around. I can see too the shape of Mrs. Taverner as she stoops before me. And I can see Bonnie, quite limp, as she is lifted up, the golden curls bouncing about her still face. There are livid marks on her neck, and the skin all around her mouth is smeared with my blood.

*　　*　　*

Bonnie didn't die.

She was stronger even than I thought.

At this moment she is in the care of the local authorities. I don't know where. I don't want to know. I don't care any more. The fact that she still lives seems of little importance to me now.

When Kate leaves in the next few minutes I shall be totally alone. Right now she sits, staring into space, picking idly at the fingers of a cotton glove. Her eyes look vacant, the pupils dilated. She seems, nowadays, to be under a permanent state of sedation—how much of it comes from within, and how much of it comes from the doctor's prescription, I don't know. But some means of withdrawal were necessary for her, I know; she couldn't possibly go on as she was; I recall so vividly how she threw herself on Lucy's coffin at the funeral, and had to be dragged back, forcibly.

She blames me for Lucy's death, I think, in spite of what her knowledge and her intelligence tell her. In the police station that day she came at me in such a fury of despair, slicing my cheek with the stone in her ring. The ring that I gave her. I shall keep the scar. It will go with the ones that Bonnie gave me.

Now she gets up, paces. I watch her for a moment and then turn away to follow her progress in the mirror. She doesn't look at me at all. She just wanders back and forth from the window to the door, waiting, totally out of reach a few feet away.

My eyes flick to my own reflection for a second or two, and I'm suddenly aware—like seeing an old friend after a passage of time—of the passing years, the change in me. I would never go grey, you told me once—Do you remember? Oh, Kate you were wrong about so many things.

I move round in my chair, away from my image, and look at her suitcases all packed and standing by the hall door. She will go to a cousin in the North—someone she hardly knows, really. I feel useless.

"Shall I take your suitcases downstairs, ready for the taxi—?" I ask.

She shakes her head, no, the driver will come and collect them. "You mustn't go to any trouble," she says dully.

"It's no trouble . . ." How formal I sound. We're like strangers.

She sits again, waits, and I wait with her. I trace the bite-marks on my hand, little dark-red semi-circles.

The first two fingers of my right hand have only intermittent searing pain in the way of sensation now. The surgeon told me they'll never be any better and that I must be prepared for them to be amputated. Well, they're no good to me as they are. And they're ugly to look at;—and uglier still for being so completely useless. It'll probably be better when they're gone—I've got to get used to working without them, and at the moment they're just in the way. I have to admire the surgeon's work, though; the bones were so badly crushed and it's a wonder he was able to save them this far. He is a very thorough man—but no match for Bonnie.

Kate hasn't mentioned Bonnie. She won't speak of her. Though she *has* accepted the truth about her—I think—as far as she is able to accept the truth about anything. And that's something else she can't forgive me for; the fact that I made her *face* the horror—leaving her with nothing.

And it's true—she has nothing. Nothing at all. You can see it in her face. She is lost, destitute, bereft of everything that gave meaning to her life. Once she had everything. We had everything.

I will go to her. Now. Perhaps there's still a chance for us. Catastrophe brings other people together—why should we two be separated by it?

"*Kate . . .*"

I wait but she doesn't answer. She twists the glove in her hand.

"Kate . . ."

I reach out; my left hand brushes her shoulder. She flinches, moves away a fraction of an inch, almost imperceptible, but enough.

"Don't," she says. Then shakes her head. "I'm sorry . . ."

No chance. No chance at all, and I retreat back into my own emptiness.

And now the taxi-driver is here, insistently ringing the doorbell. There is no more time for talk. She gets to her feet, picks up her bag.

I move forward. "Shall I answer it—?" It'll be the last thing I can do for her. She nods, then turns away, avoiding my eyes. She knows as well as I do that this is the last ending. She looks in the mirror, lifting nervous hands to twitch at her hair. I go on into the hall and open the door.

Bonnie stands there.

I catch her in the act of stretching up, on her toes, reaching to press again at the bell-button. She stops, looks up at me, drops her hand. From behind me I hear Kate's gasp.

"*Bonnie . . . !*"

Bonnie stands looking past me at Kate. I stand between them, glancing from one to the other.

"*. . . Mummy . . . ?*"

There is an anxious, pleading note in Bonnie's voice. Her eyes glisten with tears and her lip quivers. On her throat I can see the bruises left by my hands. She wears a dress I haven't seen before. *How did she get here? Did she come here alone? How?*

Kate is staring, incredulous. She begins to weep, sinking to her knees, her bag falling from trembling fingers. Tears streaming down her cheeks she lifts her thin arms, her hands reaching out. She speaks again, the word full of the sound of wonder.

"Bonnie . . ."

"Mummy . . ." Bonnie's voice again, tiny, hardly there, and then Kate's—sounding as if it is torn from her.

"Oh, my baby! . . . ! My baby . . . ! Come to me . . ."

Bonnie runs past me and throws herself into the waiting arms. Kate rises, turning from me, holding Bonnie tight against her, Bonnie clinging as if she'll never let go. She looks at me over Kate's shoulder. Such big, blue eyes. I can feel the hair at the nape of my neck rising . . .

She gives me a little smile.

Is it of triumph? Is it happiness?

Maybe it's both.

I shall never know.